P

MW01614750

Doug Fletcher book 6

Dean L. Hovey

Print ISBNs
Amazon Print 978;0;2286;1537;8
B&N Print 978;0;2286;1538;5
LSI Print 978;0;2286;1626;9

BWL Publishing Inc.

Books we love to write ...
Authors around the world.
http://bwlpublishing.ca

Copyright 2021 Dean L. Hovey
Cover design by Michelle Lee

All rights reserved. Without limiting the rights under copyright reserved above, no part of this publication may be reproduced, stored in or introduced into a retrieval system, or transmitted, in any form, or by any means (electronic, mechanical, photocopying, recording, or otherwise) without the prior written permission of both the copyright owner and the publisher of this book.

Dedication

Chief Rick Wilson, Cambridge (MN) Police Department 1959-2006

Acknowledgements

As always, I'm indebted to a number of people who've given me support in a variety of ways. At the top of that list is always Julie, who reads early drafts, critiques the characters, provides corrections to medical details, and puts up with my endless hours on the computer. Deanna Wilson happily stepped in to help with all things horse or cop related and offered up a portion of the ending when the characters had written me into a corner (yes, they occasionally take the book places I hadn't envisioned). Clem MacIlravie helps me with gun related details and Western culture. Frannie Brozo, an archaeologist by education, helped with innumerable natural history issues and offered critique. Mike Westfall and Warren Wasescha read early proofs and offered plot and hiking technical suggestions. Natalie Lund and Anne Flagge proofread and critiqued.

Thanks to Siri Jeffrey and Jude Pittman of BWL for their help and support.

This book is a work of fiction. The people, events, and places are creations of the writer's imagination or are used fictionally. Any resemblance to actual events, places, or people is accidental and unintended.

"On average, 6 people die in national parks every week."

A. J. Willingham, CNN April 24, 2019

Prologue

Steve Palmer was as cold as he'd ever been, having made the rookie hiker's mistake of not dressing in layers and not wearing a base layer of clothing to wick moisture away from his skin. He'd hiked hard, working up a sweat, then sat down to cool off. His body had gone from hot, to comfortable, to cool, to cold, in fifteen minutes as the relentless Black Hills wind blew in his face. Checking his watch, he was reminded of the ranger's warning to be back in camp before sunset. South Dakota twilight didn't linger this close to the winter solstice.

Dark shapes on a distant hill, bison, seemed to move in slow motion as they grazed in the thin prairie grass. Prairie dogs popped out of their holes, ducked down, then raced from one hole to another. They'd spread shrill warnings when Steve had arrived but quickly determined he was no threat. He was half a mile off the trail in a rugged part of Wind Cave National Park, far from the campground, visitor center, and cave entrance. According to the map, the nearest road was miles away. He'd read there are literally only a few places in the United States more remote than this part of western South Dakota.

A white contrail cut the sky. Dark clouds hung on the western horizon, a harbinger of forecasted snow. The wind hid the whisper of something rubbing against sagebrush behind him, then a searing pain ripped his neck. His body was jerked back, throwing his head against the ground and dazing him. Breath whistled from his torn trachea. Warm blood squirted between his fingers as he clutched his torn neck. His next breath blew bubbles and his field of vision narrowed, then went dark. His last thought was, "*What happened?*"

His heart beat another ten times before it, like his brain, ran out of oxygen and stopped.

Chapter One

At our wedding reception, my new wife, Jill, had dropped the bombshell that we were invited to spend Thanksgiving at her parents' South Dakota ranch. The trip was announced as a holiday with family and a chance for us to meet the neighbors. It turned out to be a series of tests of whether I was a worthy husband for Al and Molly Rickowski's fifty-one-year-old daughter. If I'd known about the hidden agenda, I would've come up with some excuse to stay at my National Park Service assignment at Padre Island National Seashore in Texas.

Besides the "worthiness" assessments, including skills shooting a pistol and riding a horse, the strangest turn of events was when I was summoned by the National Park Service to investigate what was thought to be an accidental fall at Devils Tower National Monument. The second strangest turn was when Jill, a long time National Park Service ranger and park superintendent, was sworn in as a law enforcement ranger under an obscure and seldom used National Park Service regulation that allowed experienced rangers to be sworn in to fill open law enforcement positions.

The Devils Tower fall I'd been dispatched to investigate turned out to be a murder rather than an accident. The investigation ended with Jill's baptism under fire. After teary good-byes we flew back to Corpus Christi and our "home" National Park Service assignment. We dragged our bags into our rental house on Mustang Island after multiple flight connections from Rapid City to Corpus Christi. A blizzard delaying all flights out of Minneapolis for half a day added to the misery of an extraordinarily long day.

I hit snooze when the alarm rang at five. Jill amazed me by hopping out of bed and dashing into the bathroom. While Jill sang in the shower, I stumbled downstairs and started a pot of coffee. I was staring into a steaming mug when Jill walked downstairs. She always looks ready to take on the world as soon as she steps out of the shower. She ran her fingers through her damp hair as she walked into the kitchen in her National Park Service (NPS) green and gray uniform.

She poured herself coffee and put a slice of bread into the toaster. "Do you want me to take out your peanut butter too, or do I only need to take out the creamy?"

One of our newlywed discoveries was that she liked creamy peanut butter and I liked chunky. The compromise was having jars of both.

"Yeah, I'll make some toast when I wake up."

The toaster popped and Jill was humming a tune I didn't recognize while spreading peanut butter and prickly pear cactus jam on her toast. She sat across from me, turned on the television and switched to a local news broadcast.

"You know, you don't have to be happy every morning. You're in a freshly pressed uniform, your face is rosy, and...you're humming."

"I guess someone got up on the wrong side of the bed."

I glared at her, but instead of a frown, I got a smile with dimples that always melted my heart. "Put a slice in the toaster for me. I'll be back in five."

"If you're going to be grumpy, put your own toast in when you come down and spread your own peanut butter on it, too." I leaned around the corner to respond but got caught short. "If you say, 'yes dear' you'd better be prepared to catch a coffee mug in your teeth."

I reflexively protected my ribs, where Jill had planted an elbow after every 'yes dear' our entire Thanksgiving trip. I went upstairs, showered in what was left of the lukewarm water after Jill's lengthy shower, toweled off, put on my uniform. Not that a uniform was required in my position as an investigator, but because it was our first day back and I didn't know who might be around the headquarters building.

My coffee mug had been topped off, there was toast, spread with crunchy peanut butter on a plate and a newspaper was spread on the dining room table.

"Anything in the news?"

Jill looked up from the sudoku puzzle. "The usual stuff. There was a police-involved shooting after a burglary and another ICE sweep for undocumented people at a restaurant. Nothing new."

The coffee and toast infused me with enough energy to put my plate and mug in the dishwasher. I took my Sig 220 pistol off the closet shelf and clipped it to my belt. Jill was struggling to pin her badge to her uniform shirt, so I helped, only then remembering she'd been sworn in as a law enforcement ranger and had been issued the larger badge worn by sworn officers.

"Are you going to stay on the dark side?" I asked, referring to her transfer to law enforcement.

"I guess that depends on Matt. If he needs an interpretive ranger more than a park cop, I guess I'll be guiding tours and selling brochures. In the meanwhile, hand me my Browning. I'll wear it to the Park."

Jill drove to the park headquarters in a new pickup she'd purchased before we left for South Dakota. We were waved past the entrance hut by a ranger who looked like she was a teenager. It was brisk, and we'd worn jackets to ward off the cool, damp December wind coming off the Gulf of Mexico. We hung the jackets in my office and walked to the superintendent's office down the hallway. I could hear Matt Mattson's voice before we got to his door. Rachel Randall, who'd been shot in the arm during a bungled arrest in the weeks before our South Dakota trip, was sitting in Matt's guest chair. Her arm was out of the sling she'd worn before our departure, and she sounded happy and upbeat.

Rachel got up and moved to a chair farther in the corner. "Ah, the newlyweds have returned from their happy holiday with the cowboy in-laws. How'd your horseback ride go, Doug? Did you manage to stay in the saddle?"

I'd told Rachel of my hatred and mistrust of horses and she reveled in the knowledge that my father-in-law had planned to take me out riding.

Jill jumped in before I could answer. "Daddy found an old, sway-backed nag for Doug to ride. She could barely walk, much less buck him off."

Matt shook his head. "Rachel, give me a few minutes with Jill and Doug so I can explain some of the changes."

The gleam in Rachel's eye told me something I was about to hear was going to rankle me. I put my hand on her arm as she passed. "How's your rehab going?"

"Okay. Getting shot hurts a lot more than I would've guessed, and the recovery isn't overnight."

"But you're okay and back on duty?"

She nodded, then took a step out the door. I felt her hand tug on my shoulder, so I followed her into the hallway. She glanced around, like she had a juicy rumor. Seeing no one, she threw her arms around me and hugged me. "Doug…"

I patted her back. "What's up?"

She released the hug and stared at her shoes. "I talked with the CCPD chief while you were gone. They completed the shooting board of review and determined the discharge of our firearms was justified."

"I was sure that would be the decision."

"Doug, part of the determination…your justification, was that my life was in imminent danger. The board said if you hadn't shot, I would likely have been hit by additional shots from the gunman's automatic weapon. The chief said with all the bullets being fired around…I might not have survived until the ambulance got there."

I put my hands on her shoulders. "He has no way of knowing…"

"Shh. Ron and I want to take you and Jill out to supper this week…as thanks."

"You don't…"

Rachel cut me off and leaned around the corner, interrupting a conversation between Matt and Jill. "Hey, Jill, Ron and I are taking you and Doug out to Landry's. Is tonight open?"

"I don't know of anything going on."

Rachel looked at me, knowing the argument was now over. "Leave your wallet home, cowboy."

I walked into Matt's office and sat in the chair, getting a "what happened?" look from Jill.

Matt opened a desk drawer and took out a sheet of paper. "I printed this out rather than forwarding it and having copies on multiple computers." He pushed the sheet across his desk so both of us could read it. The sender was Matt's boss, the National Park Service regional superintendent. It said Jill was assigned to Padre Island as a permanent law enforcement ranger under the rules allowing current permanent rangers to be "transitioned" to seasonal law enforcement openings. She was transferred from Flagstaff without loss of job grade or reduction in salary.

I stopped reading after that first paragraph and gave Matt a 'thumbs up' sign. Matt put up his hand while Jill read the rest of the email. She looked at Matt. "Really? I've never heard of this program and I left Flagstaff persona non grata."

Matt looked at me. "Can you give Jill and me a minute?"

I got up. "Sure." I was going to close the door, but Matt stopped me. "Guidelines suggest that office doors not be closed when a senior male ranger speaks with a junior female who reports to him."

I frowned, but Matt didn't smile. "Just wait outside the door."

I caught a hint he'd been ordered to have a private conversation with Jill, but he wanted me to listen in.

Jill didn't catch our exchange. "Really, Matt? You can't close the door with me in the office? That's the most…"

"Listen, Jill, here's what's going on. Because you're not educationally qualified to be a law enforcement ranger, I've been directed, not asked, but directed, to rectify that. Until I have appropriate documentation of your law enforcement education your file is 'lost' in a regional office. Once your qualifications are documented, your file will be located, I'll put the transcripts into your file, and I'll process the paperwork to have you reclassified as a 'permanent' law enforcement ranger."

"This is beyond stupid! I'm not going back to school to get a law enforcement degree. Just let me be an interpretative ranger and leave it be."

"Jill, I got that email and had several calls from…senior National Park Service managers. We're not being offered an option. You're a law enforcement ranger and I've been told to figure out how to make the documentation right. I did some research, and because you already have a bachelor's degree in forestry, all I need is a couple law enforcement classes on a transcript to put in your file and all the bases will be covered."

"All the asses will be covered."

"There are letters of commendation in your file crediting you with contributions to several National Park Service investigations. The Crook County Sheriff and Rapid City FBI Special Agent in Charge each sent a letter I scanned and emailed to everyone in my chain of command, including the Secretary of the Interior."

14

I heard a drawer open and papers shuffle. Matt reached around the door and handed me a copy of the letters before returning to his chair. The room went silent, and I assumed Jill was reading the same documents that had been handed to me. I expected a brief letter of thanks from the sheriff. He'd written a three page letter, enumerating Jill's role in the investigation, crediting her with saving the life of his deputy by pulling him off I-90, and detailing the circumstances that led to the shootout when we'd gone to arrest the murder suspect. "At great personal risk Ranger Fletcher stepped from a protected position and fired at a well-armed suspect who was shooting at law enforcement personnel, until he was no longer a threat."

The letter from the FBI SAC was nearly as glowing. The letter from the sheriff was great, but a letter in a National Park Service file from the FBI was golden and would probably make Jill "bullet-proof" from National Park Service political attacks and budget cuts as long as she wore the uniform.

I heard Jill flipping pages, followed by silence. Her voice softened. "Okay, Matt, how are you going to accomplish that?"

I heard a drawer squeak. "You're enrolled in a night class."

"You've enrolled me in a class without even asking me?"

"Yes. You're taking Criminology 101. Here's your textbook, here are the notes from earlier this quarter, this is a test you'll fill out and turn in to the professor the first night, and here's the class syllabus."

"No way! I'm not going to sit in a classroom with a bunch of kids who are young enough to be my children. Hell, they're probably young enough to be my grandchildren!"

Matt's voice softened. "You know the National Park Service is a quasi-military organization. The job grades have military equivalents, and the hierarchy looks like an Army division. I'm your direct supervisor, your commander. I'm ordering you to attend this class."

"And if I refuse."

"Take it easy. I've spoken with the professor and he's letting you take the class pass/fail. The semester is nearly over, and you'll be in class with the person who took the notes I gave you."

I heard Matt pick up the phone and punch in a number. "Come in now, please."

Jill was mad. "Damn it Matt, this is bullshit! I've never heard of anyone being ordered to take a class. Tell you what, you can have my badge! Don't let it cut you when you shove it…"

I stepped into the office as Matt put up his hands. "Just wait a minute."

I heard approaching footsteps and looked down the hallway. Mandy, Matt's southern belle

16

wife, was walking toward me, smiling. "Welcome back to Texas, Doug."

Mandy pecked me on the cheek and walked into Matt's office. Matt walked out and steered me into the hallway. He closed the door and leaned against it, then blew out a breath. "I hope this works."

"Who's taking the class with Jill?"

"Mandy."

I laughed. "Really!" Matt nodded and I clapped him on the shoulder. "You sly dog."

"I've got to tell you. Jill's job isn't the only one on the line. I was told to make this work, or I'd be given a snow shovel and assigned to Isle Royale National Park in the middle of Lake Superior."

"Isle Royale is pretty."

Matt gave me a disgusted look. "That's not funny. Can you picture Mandy in a parka and mukluks shoveling the sidewalk? Hell, you have to take a boat to get to a store!"

Jill started arguing, then the voices were muffled. The door opened and Jill walked out.

Matt put out his hand. "Friends?"

Jill gave me a look, then brushed aside Matt's hand and hugged him. "Using Mandy was underhanded."

"Believe me, I had to dig deep to come up with some way of talking you into this. My alternatives were limited."

I shook my head. "I'm confused. Why is Mandy taking Criminology?"

17

Mandy smiled. "Rachel stayed with us after you guys shot it out with the bad guys at the hobby store. I was curious about what you guys were into, so she filled me in and suggested I take a class. I signed up to audit the class in October."

"You're thinking about going into law enforcement?"

Mandy laughed. "Oh, heavens, no. We live in an insular environment, and I've never been exposed to the seedy underside of society. Nothing I've learned has made me interested in becoming a cop." She paused. "But I understand what you're living through a lot better."

Jill sniffled and wiped her nose with a tissue. "What nights do we have class?"

Mandy smiled. "Mondays and Thursdays. They're actually very interesting."

Jill looked at me. "You do realize this is going to cost you?"

I pointed a finger at my chest. "Me?"

"You and Matt are taking us out for supper before every class."

Matt's eyes went wide. "We are?"

Mandy smiled. "You told me to promise her whatever it took to get her into the classroom." She looked at me. "And you are going to buy her the nicest Christmas present she's ever had."

"I am?"

Mandy put on her best disarming smile. "Yes, you are. And I'm going to help you pick it out."

The sparkle returned to Jill's eyes and she nodded. "Remember, I don't want anything with a big rock on it...but Mandy pointed out that a bunch of small gems are just as nice. My birthstone is a sapphire."

Mandy nodded. "And they're nearly as expensive as diamonds."

"I just bought engagement and wedding rings."

Matt leaned close. "I think you'd better suck it up. Jill's got more seniority than you, and she's carrying a gun."

Chapter Two

Rachel Randal, my Texas partner, had covered all the law enforcement roles at Padre Island National Seashore during our Thanksgiving trip. In the weeks since the South Dakota trip, Rachel, Jill, and I had fallen into a routine rotation of one person walking the campground while the other two drove the beach. Rachel and I started our morning beach patrol later than usual because we'd dealt with two male teenagers who were flirting with a female ranger who wasn't interested in their attention. The delay meant Rachel had missed her usual lunch with the other young rangers. She pulled into the visitor center lot and parked the National Park Service pickup in the reserved spot. She pulled out her cellphone to check the time.

"We got in late last night, so I didn't bring anything for lunch. Let's go to the burger place outside the park."

Rachel, who lived frugally after having an ex-boyfriend suck her finances dry for seven years, packed a lunch at home and ate in the break room. "I've got a salad in the refrigerator."

I smiled. "Only if you wrote your name and date on the container." The pilfering of lunches from the break room was a standing joke and any package lacking a name and date was considered fair game among the young seasonal rangers, many of whom were fresh out of college, paying off massive student loans, and living on a shoestring.

"It's Rubbermaid and my name *is* written on it, with indelible ink."

Rachel got out of the pickup and we walked toward the visitor center. I spotted Jill walking back from patrolling the campground on foot. I met her at the back of the parking lot.

"I'm going to the burger place for lunch. Would you like to join me?"

Jill considered my suggestion. "I haven't eaten. Can I get a salad there?"

"I'm sure they're available." I really had no idea, but I didn't want to go for lunch alone.

Jill pulled the remote out of her pocket and clicked it, unlocking her new pickup. "I'll drive."

We cruised down the entrance road, meeting only one other car. December had arrived with a cold front that thinned the crowds and brought crime to a standstill, not that there was a lot of crime in the park.

"Remind me why you bought a pickup?"

"It's what I learned to drive in, and I like sitting up high."

"I always figured you for a sporty car."

Jill glanced at me. "You've known me for two years. What in that history makes you think I'd buy a sporty car?"

"I don't know. You'd been single for years with disposable income, I just figured you'd buy something fun."

Jill shook her head. "You're full of it. Do you throw those things out just to see if you can get me stirred up?"

"The conversation gets a little thin sometimes. If I tweak you, we discuss things."

Jill pulled into the parking lot and stopped at the order kiosk in the drive-through lane. There were two cars ahead of us waiting for their orders. She looked at the menu, then glared at me. "There are zero salad options. Zero."

An upbeat voice told us to give her our order as soon as we were ready.

I leaned close to Jill's window to order. "I'll have a double cheeseburger basket with a chocolate shake."

"Would you like that small, medium, or large, sir?"

"Large, please."

Jill shook her head as she scanned the food options on the kiosk. "I'll have a single burger with extra lettuce and tomato."

"Would you like to make that a basket for an additional dollar?" The perky voice asked.

"No. Just the burger and diet cola."

The perky voice gave us our total and told us to pull ahead to the first window.

22

"Doug, how can you eat like this and not weigh three hundred pounds?"

"I have a fast metabolism. I didn't order the bacon cheeseburger." Seeing no positive response to my smart remark I added, "I'll share my fries."

We got to the window and Jill looked at me. "Your turn to buy, big spender."

I pulled out my wallet and handed Jill a twenty-dollar bill. When she held out the twenty the window was empty. We idled at the window as the car ahead of us pulled up and got their drinks. There was some discussion with the person at the window, then they were handed a number and pulled ahead into a spot reserved for cars awaiting the fulfillment of their orders.

A haggard middle-aged woman showed up at the window and Jill held out the twenty. The woman, whose nametag said "Alice – Manager" ignored the money and glanced at our badges, then at the car ahead of us.

"Are you guys cops?"

"We're Park Service Rangers," Jill replied.

I leaned across Jill, sensing the anxiety in the manager's demeanor. "We're law enforcement rangers, Federal cops. Is there a problem?"

"The woman in the car in front of you handed this note over with her money."

Jill accepted a gas station receipt. "HELP ME" was written in pencil across the back of it.

"How long before their meal will be ready?" I asked.

"We called 911 and we're hoping the cops show up really soon. I'm afraid they'll drive off if we stall too long."

A car horn beeped behind us.

The manager was frantic. "Can you guys talk to them and figure out what's going on?"

Jill looked at me with a mixture of apprehension and pleading on her face.

"How many people are in the car?"

"A woman was driving. There were two men: One in the front and one in the back."

"Call 911 and see how long it'll be before the CCPD cops respond, then stay on the phone with them. We'll check the situation inside the car." I looked at Jill, whose hands were gripping the steering wheel so hard that her knuckles were white. "Pull up to the next window and stop."

Jill stopped at the window and looked at me. "How do we do this?"

"We're going to sit here until the CCPD officers show up and we'll back them up."

Jill nodded, but her eyes were glued to the men in the car in front of us. "They're getting suspicious. I don't think they're going to hang around for their order. We need to detain them until CCPD gets here or they're going to take off."

"We're not wearing vests. If they're armed, this could get ugly fast."

"The woman just started the car." Jill let out a deep breath. "How do we do this without vests?"

"The two guys are watching the front door. Pull right and stop by their bumper. As soon as you stop rolling, I'll jump out and put a gun on the guy in the front seat. You cover the guy in the back. Switch your safety off and keep your finger next to the trigger, but not on it. If you see a gun, yell out. If your guy goes for a gun, shoot."

"Doug…that guy in Wyoming was shooting at cops. These guys are just sitting here."

"This might be nothing more than a bad joke gone wrong, but the woman's life might depend on us."

Jill nodded.

"We don't have to do this. We could cruise by them and wait for CCPD."

"No, I'm good." She paused. "You're right, that woman's life might depend on us."

Jill took her foot off the brake and she turned the wheel. She drove the thirty feet to the car and stopped. I had my Sig out and in both hands before the truck stopped rolling. I rushed to the passenger's door and pointed the muzzle at the passenger.

"Put your hands where I can see them!" I heard Jill yelling at the backseat occupant.

The female driver screamed, pushed her door open, and rolled out of the car. She got to her feet and ran for the restaurant door.

The guy in the passenger seat looked at my pistol and slowly raised his hands. I pulled the door open with my left hand. "Keep your hands up and step out of the car." As he stood, I could see a gun that had been under his leg. "I've got a gun on the seat up here!"

Jill's voice was filled with tension as she yelled at the backseat passenger. "Keep your hands up! Do not reach down!"

I grabbed my guy's arm and spun him, so he was facing the car. I pushed him against the car and kicked his right foot, to spread them so he was off balance. Then I bent down so I could see the guy Jill was talking to. He was looking at her, but was leaning away from the window, toward the console between the seats.

A siren wailed in the distance, followed by a second, slightly out of synch. The manager ran out the front door. "The cops are coming. They said two minutes."

I kicked my guy's left foot out and he fell. I put my knee on his back and pulled open the back door opposite Jill.

"Freeze!"

I was eye-to-eye with a guy with a shaved head and tattoos on his arms and neck. He looked at me with contempt but staring at the muzzle of my Sig had his attention. Jill pulled open the other door and took a step back.

"Get out slowly with your hands up," she said softly.

The guy continued to stare at me. "I'd do what she says. She put a whole clip into the last guy who pulled a gun on her."

The guy sneered and turned his head toward Jill. Something about her stance and intensity got his attention. He kept the attitude but stepped out and put his hands on the car.

The sirens cut out a block away, but I could see their flashers reflected in the restaurant's windows. The first cruiser blocked the front of the car and the second screeched to a stop a foot behind me. The four CCPD officers were out of their cruisers with the guns drawn.

"Fletcher? Is that you?"

"Yes," Jill and I responded in unison.

"There's a pistol on the front seat," I said, holstering my gun. "Check the console in the back."

Chapter Three

Rachel was leaning against the National Park Service pickup with her arms crossed when we pulled into the visitor center parking lot.

"Long lunch."

Jill stalked past her. "You go to lunch with him next time."

"What was that all about? Is she pissed because the burger joint doesn't serve salads?"

I motioned for her to go into the building. "Let's talk to Matt."

Rachel fell into step beside me. "You guys had a fight at lunch?"

I ignored her question and walked into Matt's office, interrupting him while reading an email.

He turned the screen away so we couldn't see it. "What's up?"

"Jill needs a vest and something other than her Browning peashooter if she's going to be in law enforcement."

Matt and Rachel were surprised by the intensity of my demands.

Matt grabbed a pen and made a note. "What brought this on?"

I told them about our lunch experience. Then added that the woman had run from the restaurant during the confrontation.

Rachel was concerned. "That's why Jill said I should go to lunch with you next time."

I took a deep breath, letting the adrenaline seep away. "Yeah. Jill was unprepared to deal with the instant stress, intensity and instant let down."

Matt looked past me, at his door. "Is Jill out there?"

I looked over my shoulder. "I think she's walking off the adrenaline."

Matt pulled a sheet of paper off his printer and handed it to me. "Rachel, would you find Jill and bring her here?"

I sat in one of Matt's guest chairs and took a breath. "What is this?"

"Read it for yourself. Would you like a cup of coffee?"

I'd already read the letterhead from the regional National Park Service and was bracing myself for the text. "Are you sure I won't need more than coffee to deal with whatever this says?"

Matt gave me a non-expressive look. "Black, if I remember correctly." He walked out the door.

The letter was an informational request, asking if I was available for a temporary investigative assignment at Wind Cave National Park. A hiker's body had been found near a trail and the coroner had left the death determination "open pending further investigation."

Matt set a ceramic mug in front of me and sat down. "What do you think?"

"I don't know enough to think anything. Where's Wind Cave?"

Matt spun his computer screen around and clicked on an icon he'd had open. A map of western South Dakota appeared, with a red teardrop south of the I-90 interstate. He shrunk the map so city names showed up. "It's south of Rapid City. That's not far from Spearfish, right?"

"Rapid City is the regional airport," Jill said from the doorway. Rachel pushed past her and sat in Matt's second guest chair.

"Grab a chair out of the break room, Jill."

Rachel leaned over Matt's desk, looking at the map. "Where's Jill from?"

"Her parents have a hobby ranch outside Spearfish."

Rachel smiled. "I bet you could ride a horse from their place to Wind Cave National Park."

She didn't want to pass up a chance to needle me about my in-laws being ranchers who wanted me, their only son-in-law, to learn to ride.

Jill pulled in a chair and closed Matt's door. "Wind Cave is about ninety miles from my folks' place."

Matt handed Jill the printout I'd read. "I have a National Park Service request for assistance investigating the death of a hiker in Wind Cave National Park."

Jill scanned the email. "And..."

Matt leaned back in his chair. "Rachel and I talked about who'd cover here if you and Doug went to South Dakota."

Rachel leaned back in her chair. "My mom's flying down from Indiana to spend Christmas with me. Matt's other new law enforcement ranger will be here next week. We can cover the park while you're in South Dakota."

I could tell Jill had mixed feelings. Her parents had invited us for Christmas, but it had been only weeks since we'd been there for a Thanksgiving/wedding reception feast with their neighbors. We'd declined the offer to join them for Christmas, using the excuse that it was our turn to be on duty at the park after being gone for the Thanksgiving holiday. In truth, neither of us were in a hurry to rush back to their ranch and the familial stress.

Jill looked at me. "What do you think?"

I looked at Matt. "Can Jill get the time away, and is the National Park Service paying for Jill to fly there for an investigation?"

31

Matt thought about the question and looked at Jill. "You're through with the Criminology course, right?"

"We had the final last Thursday. The grades should be posted today or tomorrow. Mandy and I took it pass/fail, so I'm sure we've passed, although it's not on a transcript you can put in my file yet. I'm signed up for Research Methods in Criminal Justice starting in January."

Matt opened a lower drawer in his desk, took out a flat white box and slid it across the desktop to Jill. She pulled back the flaps and flipped open the top exposing a new Glock pistol.

"That's your assigned service weapon. It's 9mm, which I understand is what most female rangers prefer."

Jill took it out of the box. Carefully pointing it away from us, she pulled back the slide. It locked open. She checked the chamber to make sure it was empty, then released the slide.

"The National Park Service is issuing Glocks now?" I asked.

"That's what I was told when I checked into it. Is there something wrong with them?"

I shook my head. "Not at all. They're light, low maintenance, and nearly indestructible. I wasn't aware we'd moved from the Sig Sauer."

Matt watched Jill remove and reinsert the magazine. "I'd like your Training Officer to take you to the CCPD range so you can qualify with the Glock. Then buy a holster. I ordered a soft vest for you, but it takes longer to get a vest than a pistol."

I looked at the gun and then at Matt. "I'd prefer her to carry something with a little more punch, like a .40 caliber."

Jill slid the box onto her lap. "Mr. Training Officer, sir, I'd rather shoot a caliber I can handle and hit the target with than have a heavy clunker like your Sig. I seem to recall an incident where my performance with the 9mm was just fine."

I nodded, recalling her marksmanship when a gunman was shooting at us while running for cover. Jill had emptied her pistol, trying to protect us and other law enforcement people. The shooting investigation team determined that she'd hit the running man with every shot she'd fired. I knew I'd lost this argument.

"Sure, we'll go to the range and get her qualified. Does that mean she's going with me to South Dakota?"

"The email didn't specifically request her, but I have some latitude in determining assignments, and if I approve the air travel no one's going to argue about sending two experienced investigators as long as it's in my budget."

"Is it in your budget?" I asked.

Matt smiled. "Because I was given funding to add two law enforcement rangers in October, and since one of them isn't arriving until next week, I've got a little money to spare. It's not like I'll get any points for saving a couple thousand dollars, and what usually happens is the accountants see unspent money at the end of the year and reallocate it."

Rachel nudged me with her elbow. "Giddy up, cowboy."

Matt pushed the email printout to me. "The Wind Cave park superintendent's phone number is in the email. Give him a call, then make plane reservations."

Matt looked at Jill. "You'd better call your folks and tell them you'll be at the ranch for Christmas."

I shook my head. "Maybe we'll find a motel in Rapid City or Custer, closer to the park."

Jill shook her head. "If Daddy finds out you chose a motel instead of staying at the ranch, he'll strip you naked, tie you behind a horse, and drag you across the prairie."

Matt smiled. "That paints a picture in my mind. Doesn't seem worth it to avoid a squeaking bed spring."

I frowned at Jill who grinned. "I might've mentioned the squeaky bed incident to Mandy." She batted her eyes at me, like I've seen Mandy do to Matt when she was feigning innocence. "I hope you don't mind."

"Yes, dear."

I leaned aside quickly anticipating the elbow thrust that narrowly missed my ribs.

Matt's eyes went wide. "You've got to stop doing that, Jill. People think you two are having problems."

"Tell Fletcher to quit giving me his snarky 'yes dear' response."

Rachel was almost in tears, holding back her laughter. "Gawd, Doug, I've never seen you move so fast. And, Jill, that elbow is a deadly weapon."

I picked up the email and stood up. "I'm going to call the Wind Cave park superintendent. Would you like to join me, Mrs. Fletcher?"

Jill got up and let me pass. "I'd be happy to, Mr. Fletcher."

* * *

I closed my office door after Jill walked in, and I wrapped her in my arms. "You did great at the burger joint. I was proud of you."

Jill rested her head on my shoulder and the tension in her muscles slowly relaxed. "I was scared shitless. I mean, even more than when we were in Wyoming."

"You didn't have time to think about the situation in Wyoming. Here, you were staring into the vacant eyes of some gangbanger with time to think about what might happen and how you'd have to respond."

"I have never seen anyone with that much hatred in their eyes. It's like he was the devil, and it got to me."

"That's what he wanted to do; get into your head. He was getting ready to go for a gun and he was betting that he'd psyched you out and it'd cause you to hesitate."

"Really?"

"One second of hesitation and a second of your reaction time, and he would've put a bullet into you."

"I'm not ready for this. I'm going to give Matt the badge, and I'll stay here while you go to South Dakota."

"Listen up, rookie. You're having the self-doubt every new cop feels. That's why you're paired up with a training officer, so you can learn from your mistakes and grow."

"I don't have to put up with this if I'm leading tours and answering questions in the visitor center."

"You're good. No, you're the most seasoned rookie I've ever worked with. You have maturity, bearing, you can shoot, and you don't take shit from anyone. Those are all the things a good cop has to learn, and you've already got them."

Jill leaned out of my embrace. "Thanks for the pep talk."

"You may suffer a little PTSD."

"Nightmares."

"Worse. Don't let it get inside your head. If you do, it could make you hesitate at the wrong moment. Be confident and assertive. Those are the qualities that'll put you in control of a situation and might keep some cocky kid from thinking he can stare you down or pull a weapon before you can react. And don't ask a suspect to do something, order him to do it."

Jill sat in my guest chair. "Got it. Call South Dakota and see what's going on."

I dialed the telephone number in the email and was surprised when it was answered on the first ring.

"Superintendent Ostberg, how can I help you?"

"I'm Doug Fletcher, a National Park Service investigator from Texas. My superintendent asked me to call you about a suspicious death."

"Fletcher?"

"That's right, Doug Fletcher. I'm putting you on speakerphone. I've got another law enforcement ranger in my office too. Say hello, Jill."

"Superintendent Ostberg, I think we met at Lake of the Ozarks a few years ago. I was Jill Rickowski then."

"Jill Rickowski? Last I heard, you were in Flagstaff. Oh, and please call me Chris."

"Yes. I moved to Padre Island National Seashore, and I'm a law enforcement ranger now."

"Were you two investigating the Devils Tower fall?"

"Yes," we said in unison.

There was a pause, and I heard a door close. "I'm not sure what's going on here justifies your level of expertise, but someone up the chain of command thinks otherwise."

Jill leaned close to the speaker. "Don't tell anyone, but this is all a ruse for us to come back to South Dakota. My parents live on a Spearfish ranch and they've invited us for Christmas."

Ostberg laughed. "I'm not sure if that's an invitation or a sentence. The forecast for the next ten days is bitter cold interspersed with blizzard conditions. Given a choice, I'd rather be in Texas."

"Tell us about the hiker's body you recovered."

"Well, it's rather convoluted. We shut down the campground water and send most of the seasonal rangers home in the winter because frankly, no one camps here in the winter and the visitors drop to near nothing. The campground was empty except for one pop-up camper that'd been in the same spot for over a week. There wasn't a vehicle with it, so we started to think it had been left behind by someone who thought they could come back to it in the spring, or that it had been abandoned. We checked the license plates and they're registered to a man from Mitchell, South Dakota. I called his house, but there was no answer. I asked the Mitchell police department to do a wellness check. They told me he'd been reported missing by his employer more than a week earlier when he didn't return from a long weekend camping trip. They'd gone into his house and found it unoccupied and without any sign of foul play."

I leaned forward. "So that put the ball in your court."

"Right. I had rangers review the campground and backcountry registrations. Steve Palmer checked in the weekend before his employer reported him missing. The rangers saw him alone, then with a woman, but then they both just disappeared. I had all my available folks check the cave and walk the hiking trails, but we didn't find anything. Then, one of my interpretive rangers who specializes in local wildlife spotted crows. At first, we thought a hunter had probably wounded a deer that stumbled into the park and died, but I sent out a team to investigate."

Jill leaned forward. "And they found two bodies."

"No. They found one body. The man's body had partially decomposed, then it had frozen and been covered with snow. My crew had to chase off an eagle who was pulling bits of flesh off the body, then they had to chip it loose from the ground before carrying it to a spot where we could get a vehicle close enough to pick it up."

"What happened to the woman?" Jill asked.

"We don't know. The pickup that towed the camper trailer into the campground was gone. We contacted the county sheriff's department who put out a bulletin. It was found in an industrial part of Rapid City without license plates, tires, or battery. The keys were in the ignition."

"What's your theory?" I asked.

"I think the woman took the truck to Rapid, dumped it there and had someone pick her up."

"What was the man's cause of death?"

"The coroner couldn't tell. He had water, food, and a blanket. There was blood on his clothing, but there wasn't any skeletal trauma the coroner could point to as a cause of death. No blunt force trauma to the head. No obvious gunshot or stab wounds. No broken bones. It's like he just curled up and died."

"Hypothermia?" I asked.

"Maybe. Or maybe an alien spaceship took a blood specimen and left him."

I laughed. "No, the UFOs usually run weird sex experiments and then leave the people behind alive, but with no memory of the exact events."

Jill rolled her eyes. "Did he have a backcountry hiking permit?"

"We didn't find one. If he'd planned to stay on the trails, he didn't need one."

"Do you have a record of who the woman was?" Jill asked.

"No. Palmer checked into the campground alone and only listed his name."

"The woman showed up after he checked in?" Jill asked.

"We're not certain when she showed up, but it doesn't appear she arrived at the same time."

Jill looked at me and shrugged. "What do you want us to do?"

Ostberg laughed. "I'd hoped you could pull a rabbit out of the hat, Jill. We've got nothing. We went through the trailer and found clothing and food, but nothing that would point us to a murder motive or...anything."

"Were there women's clothes in the camper?"

"Yes, both a man's and a woman's clothing."

"But no purse or woman's wallet?" Jill asked.

"No purse or woman's ID. No ID of any kind on the man's body or in the trailer. Not a credit card, an ATM card, a work ID. Nothing."

"No money," I said.

"Right, no money. So, theft might be a motive."

Jill shook her head like she was out of questions. "Is the coroner running toxicology tests to check for a drug overdose or suicide?"

"I don't know. I was at the end of my television CSI expertise when he ruled out blunt force trauma, bullet wounds, and knife wounds."

I racked my brain for questions. "Did the Mitchell police know anything about Palmer other than who his employer had been? His age, girlfriend's name, friends, relatives, criminal history, did he own guns or hunt?"

Ostberg chuckled. "Fletcher, everyone out here owns guns."

"Did you find a gun in his possession or in the camper?"

"Now that you mention it, no, we didn't. I think most people keep them in their vehicles where they're more secure than in a camping trailer when you're out hiking."

I looked at Jill who shook her head. "Chris, I guess that's all the questions we've got right now. I'm going to book flights for Rapid City. I'll let you know when you can expect us."

"Us, as in both of you?"

"That's the plan."

"Great! I'm really looking forward to having more eyes on this. By the way, try to rent a four-wheel-drive pickup. You won't want to be driving around out here in a Prius or minivan."

"Is there any chance we can use a park service pickup?"

"Sure. I'll have a pickup at the airport when you arrive. I'll even make sure there's a set of chains in it."

Jill had an evil grin. "I might have to teach Doug how to mount chains on the tires. I don't think they're a Minnesotans thing."

I shut down the speaker. Jill dug out her cellphone. "I'll call Mom and let her know we'll be there for Christmas."

"A Rapid City motel sounds pretty tempting."

"Suck it up, Fletcher. We'll be sleeping in the bed with the squeaking springs."

I got up and hugged her. "I get very amorous over the holidays."

"I'll tell Mom to put saltpeter in your food."

"Using saltpeter to suppress male sex drive is an old wives' tale."

Jill got an evil grin. "I guess we'll test that out because I'm not having another breakfast discussion with my mother about the squeaking bedsprings."

Jill opened her smartphone and started punching in information.

"What are you doing?"

"Finding flights. American Airlines has a flight leaving at 8 a.m. arriving at 12:45 p.m. with one stop in Dallas. Should I book it?"

"You realize we'll have to be at the airport by 6:00."

Jill continued to punch information into her phone. "Yes."

"If there's a one stop from here to Rapid City, why did we hop all over the place and spend a whole day flying back and forth when we went home for Thanksgiving?"

Jill paused and looked up. "I had frequent flier miles to use."

"It cost me a day of my life that I'll never get back."

Jill went back to her phone and answered without looking up. "Your time is free. I saved us a thousand dollars by using my miles." She looked up. "We're departing tomorrow morning and returning in ten days."

"Ten days might be a long time in Spearfish, especially if I have to ride a horse and prove I'm worthy of being your husband again."

"You've already passed all the tests, so this trip should be less stressful."

I got up and walked to the door. "It's not like having to requalify with the pistol once a year?"

Jill shook her head. "No, once you've proven yourself, you're golden. Where are you going?"

"We're going to the CCPD pistol range to get you qualified with your new weapon."

Jill perked up. "I like shooting, especially when the government is paying for the ammo."

Chapter Four

Other than getting up in what seemed to be the middle of the night to be at the airport at 6 a.m., our flights were relatively painless. The green landscape of Texas got brown as we went north, then turned to white as we passed over Nebraska. I'd put my scarred hiking boots, warm socks, and a "real" winter jacket, one not donated to Goodwill when I left Minnesota, into a roller bag to be I checked. I'd even found a Minnesota Vikings stocking cap and a pair of insulated gloves in the bottom of a box I'd never unpacked in Arizona. Jill had a better selection of winter apparel from her years in Flagstaff, one that allowed her to dress in layers, and required a larger suitcase.

The plane to Rapid City wasn't large, so there wasn't a mob scene as we deplaned and walked to the bag claim area. Jill saw the slightly heavyset, middle-aged man in National Park Service gray and green before I spotted him. He recognized Jill and met her with a hug.

"Chris Ostberg, this is my husband, Doug Fletcher. Chris is the Wind Cave National Park superintendent."

We shook hands. His handshake was hearty and his smile genuine. "Jill, you hardly look a day older than you did twenty years ago in the Ozarks."

Jill smiled at the compliment. "And you're still a schmoozer, Chris."

Chris smiled and looked at the bag carousel. "Do you folks have more than your carry-on bags?"

I nodded as the bags started sliding down the chute. "We didn't need winter coats in Corpus Christi, so I'm praying that our bags with our winter gear made the trip with us."

Chris helped me pull our two bags off the carousel and we stepped aside. He held out a keyring to Jill. "I assume you remember how to drive in snow, Jill."

Jill tossed the keys to me. "Doug's a retired St. Paul cop and he's driven in crappier weather than I have in the past thirty years."

Chris glanced at our holsters. "They allow you to carry on the plane?"

I nodded. "We're federal law enforcement officers. It's just like having two extra sky marshals on the plane."

Chris took Jill's carryon bag and nodded to the exit. "Since we're already in Rapid City, I thought you'd want to start in the hospital morgue."

Jill glanced at me with one of her "really?" looks. "Yes, I'd like to talk to the pathologist who did the post-mortem exam."

Chris took out a cellphone and punched in a number as we walked. He had a brief conversation and closed the phone. "The pathologist will be available. I'll call the FBI office and see if the special agent in charge has time to meet with us."

Chris punched in another number, and I put my hand on his arm. "Ask Jess if he can meet us at the hospital."

Chris's eyes went wide as he listened to the phone ring. "You know the SAC?"

I nodded. "From our Devils Tower investigation."

Chris had a subdued conversation then shut down his phone. "He said he'd be happy to get out of the office for a while. He's meeting us in the morgue."

I followed Chris's pickup to the hospital, and we parked near the emergency room entrance. A black SUV with an array of antennae was already parked next to the entrance. Jill and Chris walked side by side, sharing park service stories while I lagged a step behind. I caught snippets of conversation that left me with the impression they'd been young, single, and a little crazy when they'd been posted together in the Ozarks. Then they walked through their history of National Park Service postings before they'd gone up the ladder to superintendent.

We stopped outside a set of double doors marked pathology. "They don't really advertise this as the morgue, but they have storage for a few bodies while holding them pending toxicology and release to a mortuary."

We walked into an anteroom with an empty desk. Lights were on in an office down the hallway. Beyond the office was another set of double doors that I assumed led to the morgue where bodies were stored, and post-mortem exams were conducted. Chris led us into the office where a man in blue scrubs and a surgical mask around his neck was sitting at a table. With him was a man who would've passed for a cowboy in dress and demeanor if not for the smooth skin of his face and neck. Jess Pond had slipped into western persona when he'd been posted to the Rapid City FBI office. He'd left behind his dark suits and ties for western cut shirts, blue jeans, boots, and Stetson hats. Both men stood as we walked in.

Jess smiled and shook his head. "If it isn't the Fletchers. You just couldn't stay away from the Black Hills." Jess shook Jill's hand first, then mine. "Doc Pardee, these folks are Jill and Doug Fletcher from the U.S. National Park Service. I assume you already know Chris Ostberg."

We shook hands and the doctor gestured for us to take seats around his office's round conference table. "Jess's people haven't had a lot of time to put into this investigation, so Chris said he might be able to get some investigative assistance through the National Park Service. I assume that's you two."

Jess Pond put up his hand. "Doc, Jill and Doug just led the investigation of the guy who died in the Devils Tower fall. If not for Jill's shooting ability, I think a couple of sheriff's deputies and my agents would've been wounded."

The doctor looked impressed, then froze. "I did the post-mortem on a guy Crook County was trying to arrest for murder. He'd been shot fourteen times and the sheriff swore all the gunshots were made by a woman from the National Park Service. I didn't believe him."

Jess leaned on the table. "Doc, meet Jill Fletcher, the Annie Oakley of the U.S. National Park Service."

Jill blushed and clenched her jaw. She glanced at me, now understanding why I'd shied away from taking credit for actions I'd sometimes been forced into by circumstances beyond my control.

The doctor shook his head. "He was probably mortally wounded after your third or fourth shot, but the sheriff said he was still firing at law enforcement people when he hit the ground. Jess is right, you probably saved some people from gunshot wounds, or worse."

Jill nodded, and bit her lower lip.

The doctor was close to sixty and his eyes looked tired. He reached out and put his hand on Jill's hand. "It's not as easy as it looks on television, but sometimes you're forced to make tough decisions."

Jill took a deep breath and nodded. "Thanks."

Jess looked chastised. "Jill, I'm sorry for being flippant. There are cops who got to go home and hug their kids because of what you did. You shouldn't be sad or embarrassed about that."

Jill didn't know how to respond. "Um, thanks for the letter you sent to Matt. That was very kind."

"It was well deserved. I'll bet the sheriff sent one too."

Chris had apparently not heard the story about Jill's performance at the Hulett shootout and he went from skeptical to impressed to concerned. He mouthed "Wow" when she looked at him. "So, you're here to check on our John Doe."

I nodded. "We got a short version of the report. Sounds like he died without explanation and you're awaiting toxicological reports."

Pardee opened a blue folder and pulled out sheets of paper and passed them around. "Well, not entirely without explanation. I got these reports today. They're the tox reports and they've got more information, but not answers. John Doe, or Steve Palmer as we now know him, didn't die from an overdose nor was he poisoned. He had traces of THC in his system, but probably hadn't used marijuana the day of his death. There were no measurable amounts of any street drugs, pharmaceuticals, or narcotics."

"What killed him?" I asked.

Pardee smiled. "Well, I always like to say his heart stopped beating. I think in this case I can safely say that was caused by exsanguination. He bled to death."

"Bled to death?" I asked. "He bled to death sitting alone in the middle of the prairie?"

"He wasn't alone." Pardee nodded toward the door. "Would it help if we looked at the body?"

I stood. "It might be helpful."

Jill got up reluctantly, as did Chris Ostberg. We followed the pathologist through the double doors. Pardee turned on overhead lights and pointed to boxes of nitrile gloves and surgical masks by the entrance door. We each pulled on gloves and a mask as Pardee opened a giant refrigerator and wheeled out a cart with a body covered by a sheet.

I checked on Jill, who had never seen an autopsy. She hung back near the door. I pointed toward a sink mounted in the countertop and she edged toward it, rather than approaching the body.

Pardee pulled back the sheet exposing the victim's head, neck, and naked upper torso. "The victim's face, eyes, and neck looked like they'd been shredded. The torso had been protected by a heavy jacket so the carrion eaters couldn't get to it. The muscle tissue had been mostly removed, but if you look here, at the right carotid artery, you can see that it was apparently severed in several places. I initially thought it had been cut repeatedly, but under magnification this looks more like it was transected by something sharp, like…I hate to speculate, but it looks like wounds I've seen inflicted by cougar claws."

I glanced at Jess who was shaking his head. "A cougar didn't take his wallet and cellphone."

Pardee spread the torn tissue with his fingers. "Perhaps his pockets were rifled at some point after his death. He was out in the elements for close to a week after dying. A lot of things could've happened between the moment of death and the discovery of his remains."

I thought for a second. "Well, it's not like the person who stole his wallet is going to tell anyone where he found the body." I looked at Jess. "Has there been any activity on his charge or debit cards?"

"His debit card was used last Tuesday at an ATM near the college."

"Was that in the area where his truck was found?"

"It wasn't in the immediate area, but not across town, either."

I looked for Jill. She was next to the sink, staring at the ceiling with her arms crossed. Chris Ostberg was standing next to her, bracing himself on the countertop, but looking at the corpse with curiosity.

"Jill, you should see this."

She looked at me, glanced at the body, then back to me. She shook her head.

Jess Pond had his hands jammed in his front pockets. "Is there anything else you can tell us, Doc?"

"This is massive deep tissue damage. From what's left after the birds got through, it appears the artery was entirely transected in parallel cuts. There would've been blood spurting out of these wounds with each heartbeat. He would've bled out in a minute or two at most."

I looked at Chris. "Is that consistent with what you found at the scene?"

"It had sleeted, snowed, and melted a couple times before the rangers found the body. Whatever was on the ground had washed away."

"Did you use the county or the FBI to examine the crime scene?"

Ostberg shook his head. "Neither. We thought it was someone who'd died on a hike, so we just carried the body to the nearest area we could access with a pickup."

I looked at Jess Pond, the FBI agent. "Do you have a crime scene team we could take to the death scene?"

"The South Dakota Division of Criminal Investigation office in Rapid City would be our best resource."

Pardee covered the body. "I don't want to tell you how to do your job, but there was nothing on this guy's body or coat. Not a hair, a speck of dust, or any forensic evidence. Nothing. I suspect what Chris told you is exactly true. The weather from the time of guy's death to recovery of his body took care of any evidence there might've been, and now there's snow on the ground." He looked at the superintendent. "Chris, do you think you could even find the exact spot where the body had been found?"

Chris looked embarrassed. "We didn't mark the spot and that's an area of natural prairie. I could get you in the vicinity, but I doubt my rangers could get you to the exact spot. And like Doc Pardee said, there's a layer of snow over everything right now."

I looked at Jess Pond, who shrugged. "We're focusing on finding the woman who was last seen with him. Maybe she can provide some answers."

Pardee rolled the body back into the cooler and Jill stepped forward. "Is there any chance the Santa Anas will bring a melt in the next few days?"

Jess laughed. "The forecast is for cold, followed by a low-pressure system that's supposed to dump a foot of snow Christmas Day. Welcome back to the plains."

I was lost by Jill's question. "What's a Santa Ana?"

"The Santa Ana winds sweep in from the south and we sometimes get winter days that'll bounce up to fifty degrees and melt the snow. It doesn't sound like that's going to happen." Jill looked at her watch. "It's going to be dark in an hour. I think Doug and I should go to my parents' house and come back in the morning.

Chris, can we hike out to the area where the body was found tomorrow?"

Chris led us out of the autopsy suite. "I'll talk to the rangers who made the recovery. I'm sure they'd be happy to hike to Buffalo Flats with you."

Something in the tone of his voice told me there was some mirth in his comment. "Why is that funny?"

"Well, it's going to be colder than a well-driller's butt tomorrow morning. Things are so quiet around the park I think the rangers would be delighted to go on hike with you rather than sitting around waiting for a tourist to show up." He paused. "Just to be clear, I will *not* be going with you. I have piles of paperwork."

I looked at Jess Pond's smile. "Me too. I've got a ton of year-end reports to close out. But be sure and give me a call if you've got anything going on indoors."

"How cold is a well-driller's butt?"

Jess and Chris looked at each other, both smiling. Chris said. "The overnight forecast is minus twenty, and that's Fahrenheit. The windchill will make it feel like minus forty."

Jess was still smiling. "Minus forty is the same in Fahrenheit and Celsius."

Jill glanced at me. "I brought warm clothes, but not Arctic gear. Is it going to warm up soon?"

Jess shook his head. "Maybe you've forgotten the weather patterns this time of year. It only warms up when it's going to snow. So yes, it'll warm up Christmas Day when the blizzard hits."

Shit, I thought to myself. Everyone looked at me and I had the sinking feeling that my thought had actually been said out loud. "What?"

"Do you still want to hike to the site where we recovered the body?" Chris asked. "It's a couple miles from the nearest point I can reach by pickup."

"I don't suppose you have access to a helicopter?"

Chris laughed. "Not in your dreams."

I dug out the pickup keys and threw them to Jill. "You know the way to your parents' ranch from here." I turned to the others. "Thanks. We'll see Chris in the morning."

Jill started the engine and drove out of the parking area. "You didn't give me the keys because I know the way. I'm driving because we'll get home faster."

I watched Rapid City flash past. "You know, just because the pickup has a lightbar and you have a badge doesn't mean you won't get ticketed for speeding."

"We're on duty."

"My federal instructor emphasized that unless the lights and siren were on…"

Jill glanced at me and smiled. "Who's going to ticket a cop?"

"It happens."

"They might ticket someone cynical and grumpy, like you. No one's going to ticket a cheerful smiling cop like me."

I shook my head and went back to watching the scenery flash past.

Jill was silent for a few minutes. "You are trainable. You didn't say, 'yes dear.'"

* * *

The sun set as we left the interstate and a few wispy clouds turned orange, then crimson as the twilight died. The landscape was barren brown in the pickup headlights. The only change in view was the cattle guard when we crossed onto Rickowski's ranch. Jill's parents had downsized to the small plat around their house and barn when they'd sold off the bulk of the ranch.

The lights in the kitchen were blazing and a yard light lit the driveway between the house and barn. I took the two suitcases and Jill carried the two smaller bags. I'd pulled my parka out of the suitcase, but that alone wasn't enough to fend off the biting cold wind blowing from the west. My hands, ears, and nose all hurt by the time I got in the house.

Jill's father, Al, grabbed the suitcases from me and set them aside as Molly hugged me briefly before engulfing Jill in a smothering hug.

Al shook my hand. "Glad we could have some real winter for you. It was pretty wimpy when you were here last time."

The house smelled of pine, cooking apples, and cinnamon. There was a Christmas tree in the living room with a couple dozen presents under it and decorations were set on every flat surface. We'd been preparing for Christmas before we knew we'd be in South Dakota but being in the ranch house somehow brought back childhood memories of Christmases with my parents and rooms full of boisterous relatives.

Molly put her warm hands over my ears. "You look like you're half frozen and saw a ghost."

I pecked her cheek. "Your decorating reminded me of being a kid."

"I suppose a single guy doesn't put up many decorations."

I shook my head. "Even when I was married…" I cut off that thought. "This is so homey. Thanks for having us back."

Molly smiled. "This is the first year I've dug out all the decorations in a long time. We haven't been much in the Christmas spirit the last few years and it seemed like time to kick ourselves into gear."

"She's damned near killed me," Al said, trying to look put out, but smiling. "I've had to drag dusty old boxes in from all over the place to find all this bric-a-brac. I don't know how she found places to set all the stuff."

Jill was uncharacteristically quiet as she surveyed the kitchen and living room. She stepped over to Al and hugged him, making him uncomfortable. "Daddy, we haven't decorated like this since...the accident."

"I know. Molly decided it was time to really celebrate again, especially since you two were going to be here."

A kitchen timer rang, and Molly rushed to the stove and took a pie out of the oven, filling the room with a burst of warmth and even more apple and cinnamon. "Doug, your mother is flying in tomorrow afternoon. If you guys are busy, Al and I will pick her up."

"Mom's coming here for Christmas?"

"She hadn't told you?" Molly asked.

"I knew you'd invited her when you were in Texas for the wedding, but I assumed she'd be spending the holiday with our family back in Minnesota."

Al picked up the suitcases and started toward Jill's childhood bedroom. "Molly called your mom when we heard you were coming and reminded her we'd be honored to have her join us for the holidays. Ronnie immediately accepted and called us back an hour later with her flight information."

Al set the suitcases inside the bedroom and nodded for me to follow him across the hall. He turned on the light in what had been Jill's dead brother's room. In November it had still been a dusty shrine to Junior, kept behind a closed door. All of Junior's stuff was gone and the room had been redecorated with Molly's loving touch. There were new curtains, a quilt on the bed, freshly painted walls, and a light fixture was mounted where previously there'd only been a bare bulb hanging from a cord.

I was going to comment, but Al shook his head. "We redecorated the guest room. This is where we're putting your mom."

"Very nice. I'm sure Mom will be comfortable here."

Jill was leaning against the counter watching Molly. The smell of frying pork chops mingled with the apple and pine scents. Al took a bottle of Jack Daniels out of the cupboard and poured an inch of liquor into a lowball glass. I expected him to try to talk me into having a bump with him, something I'd given up when I'd crawled out of the bottle after my divorce. Instead, he took a beer from the refrigerator, popped the top, and carried it to me, nodding toward the table.

I sat next to him and thanked him. He raised his glass toward me like he was about to make a toast. I touched the neck of the beer bottle to the rim of his glass. I expected a homey, South Dakota toast to tall pastures and fat cattle, instead he said something unexpected, "Welcome home, Son."

I was speechless, after going head-to-head with him in Texas over whether I was worthy of marrying Jill, he'd called me son. "Merry Christmas, Dad."

Jill watched the exchange and smiled. Molly put her to work mashing potatoes.

Al drank down half his drink in one swallow. "Can you tell me about the dead hiker, or is that somehow secret?"

"You probably know as much as I do. A guy was found dead out in the prairie on National Park Service land. He'd been dead a few days and they don't know how he died."

"The newspaper said his truck was found in town."

I nodded. "That's true, but no one knows how it got there and we're not really sure that's tied to his murder. It might've been a crime of opportunity, as we call them. Someone found the truck with the keys in it. Nobody was around, so they took off with it and dumped it later."

"Seems kind of odd someone would steal it in the park and dump it in town. That park is a long way from anything. I'd think anyone out there would already have a rig of their own."

Jill had been listening to us. She brought a stack of plates to the table with a handful of silverware. "That's an interesting point I hadn't considered. That would imply there was more than one person involved in taking the truck."

Al nodded, smug that he'd mentioned something we hadn't considered. He looked at Jill's holster. "What happened to your Browning?"

Jill reached down and touched the holster. Carrying a pistol had become such a regular part of her persona she hadn't taken it off when we walked in the house. "This is the Glock the

National Park Service issued to me. I left the Browning in Texas." She took it out, removed the clip, ejected the shell in the chamber, and handed it to her father, butt first.

Al turned it over in his hand. "I'll never get used to these plastic guns. I like a piece of metal in my hand." He handed it back to her. "What do you think, Doug?"

"It's a solid piece. They're reliable, accurate, and nearly indestructible. We took it to the range before we came down, and Jill was shooting as well with the Glock as she was with her Browning."

Al still looked skeptical. "Is that so, Jill?"

She put the clip back in the gun and took the holster off her belt. "It's not any better than the Browning, but it's sure a lot easier to keep clean. I put two boxes of shells through it, wiped it off, and it was ready to go. I had to field strip the Browning and clean it every time we went shooting." She put the Glock on top of the refrigerator.

Molly brought a platter of pork chops to the table. "Let's talk about something other than dead men and guns."

I smiled and got up to help carry serving bowls of green beans and potatoes. "Agreed. What would you rather discuss?"

She walked to the table next to the door and handed me a small box. "I'd like to know what's in that box. The UPS guy made me sign for it."

I checked the return address, which was a P.O. box in Corpus Christi. I peeled off a layer of brown paper, exposing the surface of a cardboard box. Inside the outer box was a layer of bubble wrap and inside that was a smaller box in Christmas wrap. I turned the box until I found a tag that said, "To Jill. From Doug."

"It appears to be Jill's Christmas present. I assume Mandy Mattson had something to do with this."

Jill sat down and smiled. "She sometimes looks a little like one of Santa's elves."

I got up and put the box under the Christmas tree and threw the wrapping in the trash. "I suppose I should check my charge card statement to see how much I spent on you."

Molly grinned. "You two are so lucky to have friends like Matt and Mandy. They're very special people."

I took a pork chop and passed the platter to Al. "Yes, Jill. Tell them about the class you're taking with Mandy."

That opening led to a whole discussion about Texas, Jill's career, how we were sent to South Dakota for Christmas and more. We took a break after supper to clear the table before cutting into the apple pie. Jill suggested that we unpack, so we retreated to the bedroom and she closed the door.

As soon as the door was closed, she hugged me. "I told you Daddy wasn't going to challenge you anymore. You've graduated to 'son'."

"I hope it sticks." I put a suitcase on the bed and the springs creaked under the weight.

"Really? I thought they were going to get a new mattress and box spring that didn't squeak every time someone sits on the bed."

Jill laughed. "You're not concerned about the squeaking when someone sits on the bed. You know we're not having any romantic interludes on that bed."

"Oh, come on."

"I am NOT having another uncomfortable breakfast discussion with my mother about the activities that made the bed squeak. I was mortified after Thanksgiving."

"But honey."

I reached out to hug her, but she slipped away and almost ran out the door. "It's time for pie! Do you want ice cream?"

Chapter Five

Not only did the bedspring creak with every motion, but the entire bed also moved when either of us rolled over. I'm sure my trip to the bathroom woke Jill. Her early morning departure for the shower rocked me and the bed springs squeaked when she stood up.

"Tell me when coffee's on," I said as she slipped out the door.

Molly must've already been up because the opening door brought in the smell of coffee that got me out of bed. I slipped on a pair of pants and walked into the kitchen rubbing my eyes. Al had the morning news on the television and was already sipping coffee. I took down a mug and poured coffee, joining Al at the table.

Molly delivered two plates with bacon and pancakes. She put her arm around me and whispered in my ear. "Pretty quiet last night. Did you give up romance for the holidays?"

Al knew what she was going to say because he had an ear-to-ear grin. Jill swept into the kitchen and got a mug of coffee. When she turned, she saw us watching her and turned to Molly, who was also grinning.

"Aw, come on you guys. This isn't about the squeaking springs, is it?"

I nodded. Molly handed Jill a plate of pancakes. "I got more of the Vermont maple syrup you like."

"That doesn't make up for giving me a bad time about the mattress noises."

I swallowed a bite of pancake. "This time it was about the lack of noises from the bedroom."

"Same difference. It's not a point of discussion. What's on the news?"

Al leaned back and looked at the television. "Cold front won't break until that low-pressure system moves in from California. I hope you two brought long underwear. You're going to need it if you're going to be outside."

Jill smiled. "I had a set in the drawer that still fit."

"Unlike Jill, I'm not the same size I was in high school. I had to order a whole new set of long underwear from a website with next day delivery."

Al laughed. "That's not something off the rack in Corpus Christi?"

"Of course they are," I kidded, "they hang them between the bikinis and sunscreen."

* * *

My cellphone rang as I was buttoning my shirt. "Fletcher."

The caller ID said FBI. "Give me your email address. We've got video from the ATM where the stolen cash card was used."

I gave Jess my National Park Service email address and hung up. Within a minute I had an email with a jpeg image of a man in a stocking cap, scarf, and dark glasses. The only discernible facial feature was a band of white skin under the glasses and above the scarf.

My phone rang again. "Well, Jess, that's pretty worthless."

Jill came over to see what we were talking about. I put the phone on speaker and pulled up the photo.

"Hi, Jess. This is Jill. You've gotta love South Dakota in the winter. There's nothing discernible in that photo. I can't even see the guy's nose."

"Well, there are a couple things we got from the picture. We've been looking for the woman who was seen with our dead guy. Well, there's a guy in the mix. No way to know if he's an accomplice, someone who stole the card from the campsite, or someone who bought the card from the woman, but we have a second person to find. The other thing is the guy's hand. He took off his glove to take the money and he's got a tattoo that shows past his cuff. We're trying to enhance that so we can take it to the local tattoo artists."

"Any headway on identifying the woman?" I asked.

"I've got a guy going to all the bars with our victim's driver's license photo around the area where the ATM was used. We're hoping a bartender will remember him. If we get a hit, we might find someone who remembers him with a woman, or we might find surveillance video with him and the woman in the bar."

Jill leaned close to the phone. "Is there anything we can do to help?"

"The one agent I've assigned is focusing on the bars near the ATM. If you guys are up for it, you could canvass the bars nearer the park, in Custer and Keystone."

"Send us his picture and we'll talk to a few bartenders."

I shut down the phone and smiled at Jill. "Oh boy! We get to do real cop stuff."

Jill slipped on a down vest. "Yeah, I remember the great success we had talking to the bartender in Moorcroft. I can hardly wait."

We kissed Molly goodbye. Al waved over his shoulder from his recliner. He wasn't interested in interrupting the news nor risking spilling the coffee in his left hand. I was one step out the door when I stopped short and groaned.

Jill turned. "What's wrong?"

"There's an inch of frost on the windshield. I hope Chris left a scraper in the glove box."

"Suck it up, Fletcher. I'll scrape my side while you warm up the truck."

Jill watched me scrape with amusement. "Why are you grumbling?"

"This is why I moved away from St. Paul."

"Give it a rest. You left St. Paul because of your divorce and drinking. You had to scrape your windshield in Flagstaff too."

"The Flagstaff frost wasn't like this; it was easy to scrape. It's twenty below zero here, and this is like scraping paint. Besides, my fingers are about ready to break off."

"Give me the scraper and get in the truck."

Jill was as cold as I was, but more stubborn. The heater started blowing warm air on the windshield and I squirted washer fluid to soften the frost.

Jill got in the truck and started shivering. "I forgot how cold twenty below feels. The Gulf cold is penetrating, but I don't have to worry about body parts breaking off."

"Your dad said it's going to warm up."

"Yeah, the day it starts to snow. That'll be so much better."

Jill slid across the seat and pulled my arm over her shoulder. "At least the truck started."

"That's not an advantage. If the engine hadn't started, we could have gone back inside to drink coffee."

* * *

I thought Devils Tower was remote, but the drive to Wind Cave National Park was long and desolate. We went south from I-90, through the town of Custer, then wound through snowy prairie and timbered ridges until we hit the sign that said we were entering the Wind Cave National Park. The road was plowed, but not well traveled. There was no entry booth collecting fees, just open prairie. We passed a herd of pronghorn antelope grazing idly on small patches of brown grass a few yards off the road before coming to the National Park Service visitors center and headquarters building. Surprisingly, there were nine cars in the visitor parking lot.

The interior of the building felt familiar with a ranger sitting behind a counter and a nook offering books about the Black Hills, the park, South Dakota natural history, and other regional features. There was a sign near an elevator to the cave showing the times various tours were offered and the age restrictions for some of the tours.

A young, blonde ranger seemed perky. "We have a few openings for the next tour."

Jill and I were dressed for South Dakota winter, foregoing our uniforms in favor of jeans, heavy coats, stocking caps, and gloves. I peeled off my Minnesota Vikings stocking cap and unzipped my coat, exposing my National Park Service badge.

"I think Chris is expecting us."

The young ranger leaned over the counter and whispered so the two visitors at the book rack wouldn't hear her. "You're the rangers investigating the death of our hiker. Chris's office is in the back of the building." She pointed to her right.

Like any National Park Service administrator, Chris Ostberg was sitting at his desk reading email on his computer, his office door open. I knocked on the doorframe, and he turned his computer screen off before greeting us.

He got up to shake our hands. "Jill and Doug, you found us."

Jill stripped off her coat and hung it on a guest chair. "I haven't been here since grade school. It seemed like we rode half a day in the bus to get here."

Chris smiled. "I'll bet the drive didn't seem any shorter. There's not a lot of scenery along the way."

I put my coat on top of Jill's. "I suppose it's more scenic in the summer. The snow and brown grass make the landscape pretty bleak."

"It greens up in summer, and there's a certain beauty to the prairie and timber. People from big cities don't appreciate it, but there's a serenity here that's hard to find in a lot of the country."

I sat in a guest chair. "We drove through Custer. I saw the county courthouse, so I assume it must be the largest city in the county."

Chris pulled his chair from behind his desk and sat across from us at a small table. "We live in Custer, and yes, it's tiny, but comfortable. People know each other and look out for each other. I imagine Jill knows that feeling of community."

Jill smiled. "Everyone looks out for each other, but snoop into each other's business. There are no secrets in a small town. I suppose there's a little café where the local ranchers gather and swap rumors and lies. The wives hang out in the churches."

"Of course, there is. The old ranchers have to go somewhere in the winter to get together. It's either a café or a bar. And yes, the wives get together at ranch houses or the churches." He paused. "I don't suppose there's anything new overnight."

"I heard from the FBI this morning. The hiker's debit card was used in an ATM near the university."

Chris perked up. "Did they get a picture of the woman he was with?"

Jill let out a breath. "A man used it, and his face was covered."

Chris looked confused. "Not the woman?"

"The face was well covered, but I'd say we're 99 percent sure it was a man."

"So, how did he know the PIN to go with the debit card?"

I thought about that for a moment. "He must've gotten it from the owner somehow. The ATMs usually freeze up and keep the card if you make multiple incorrect attempts. The FBI has the victim's driver's license photo and they're showing it to the bartenders in the area where the truck was found. They hope someone will recognize him and they'll be able to look at security video to see if he was with someone."

Jill jumped in. "Jess asked us to check with the bars in Custer and Keystone, since they're closest to the campground.

"That's a short list," Chris replied.

"Do you have a list of people who were in the campground when he was there?" I asked. "We'd like to call them. Someone might remember the woman, or better yet, have a picture with her."

"I'll call the campground manager. She can see when he checked in and who else was here. That might be quite a few names."

Jill nodded. "I've learned that police work is often hours of boredom followed by seconds of terror."

I closed the office door and sat at the table. "I'm sure you don't want to advertise this, but there's a chance the woman is still in the park."

Chris leaned back. "I've accepted that as a possibility, but I've been trying to ignore it until a body showed up or she was located alive somewhere."

"You said your rangers had been checking the trails and hadn't noted any crows or other carrion eaters hanging around a carcass. Is it possible she's somewhere in the cave?"

73

Chris looked reflexively at the door to make sure it was closed. "I hate to even hear a whisper of that."

I felt he was holding something back. "You've had people lost in the cave before."

"We've had a couple kids lag behind the tour groups or wander off the trails."

Jill nodded. "But you've always found them quickly."

"They're usually yelling because they're scared and disoriented in the dark."

"But not always?" I asked.

Chris waved his hand. "I've heard stories about people who've wandered off and been lost for days, but they're old anecdotes. That's never happened while I've been here."

"But it's possible?"

Chris leaned on the table. "Doug, there are one hundred fifty miles of cave that have been explored and documented. Our tour groups don't get into more than a couple miles of it. So yes, it's possible for someone to wander off. It's pitch black, I mean 'can't see your hand in front of your face dark. If someone wandered away without a light, they could easily be lost until we realize they are missing, and our rangers find them."

I leaned back. "Let's say this woman walked away from a tour group. How long would it be before someone noticed?"

"It's impossible. The tour groups aren't that large. Tickets are sold so we know exactly how many people are touring. The guides do a headcount before leaving, they watch the guests as they lead the tour, and they do a headcount again before they exit the cave. They would know someone was missing."

"Is the tour entrance the only access to the cave?" Jill asked.

"It's the only modern access. There's the namesake wind hole that blows in and out as the barometric pressure changes, but it's pretty small and no one uses that for access."

I sensed equivocation. "But someone *could* get in there."

"That's how the original explorers got access to the cave, but it's not big enough to walk in and it's not lighted inside. No one's gone in that way in a hundred years."

"Do your rangers check inside that entrance regularly?" Jill asked.

"No. Like I said, no one goes in there. You'd have to crawl in on your hands and knees..." Realization swept Chris. "You want me to send someone in to check that access point."

I gave Chris my best stern look. "I'd like you to do that, and to have rangers check as much as possible of the rest of the cave."

"That would take weeks. I'd have to send teams in with climbing gear, water, and food to get back to some of the remote parts of the cave."

"Are there steep drops where someone without a light might fall and be disabled?" Jill asked softly, playing good cop to my bad cop.

Chris slapped his hand on the table. "Son of a bitch. For all we know that woman could be sitting in a Rapid City restaurant sipping coffee and eating a doughnut."

"Or she could be lying dead at the bottom of a cliff inside the cave," I countered. "We can't assume she left the park alive."

Jill nodded. "It's Schrodinger's cat."

"What?" I asked.

"Schrodinger put a cat in a box, then posed the question, is the cat alive or dead? There's no way to know until you open the box. Until then the answer is 'yes,' the cat is either dead or alive. So, the answer to our question is, 'yes,' the woman either is, or isn't inside the cave and we won't be able to say she is or isn't until we open the box."

"C'mon guys. I've got a winter crew. All my seasonal rangers are off until spring. I'd have to pull everyone in to search for a woman who's probably...well hell, she could be anywhere else in the country. Let's face it, she could be anywhere else in the world!"

"But she could be lying somewhere in the cave." Jill countered.

I put up my hand. "Don't we think someone would've noticed the smell of decomposition if they were anywhere near a dead body?"

Chris shook his head. "It's fifty-four degrees inside the cave year 'round. I suspect something dying in there wouldn't decompose. It's like a morgue."

"No," I replied. "Autolytic decomposition begins virtually as soon as the blood stops circulating. The bugs in your gut start eating the tissue and the buildup of carbon dioxide causes the fluids in the body to become acidic, speeding the process along. I assume there are other bacteria and mold in the cave that would aid the decomposition process. I suppose insects would get in on the feast in the summer if the body isn't too deep in the cave. Flies and beetles seem to come out of nowhere whenever I've been around a body outside of a lab."

"We're assuming she fell and died," Jill noted. "How long has she been missing? Is there any chance she's starving to death?"

Chris closed his eyes. "It's been like five days since she was last seen. There's no water in the cave, so unless she carried in a canteen, she's in deep trouble." He paused. "What are you two doing tomorrow? Are you spelunkers?"

"I've got a bad knee and crawling around in a cave would be against medical advice."

Jill looked apprehensive. "I'm not claustrophobic, but the thought of being underground in complete darkness…it's not on my bucket list."

"I'd team you up with Colleen, one of my most experienced cave people. We've got gear and everything you'd need."

I smiled. "You go on the cave search, and I'll show the victim's picture to bartenders."

"Remind me how much cave we're talking about," Jill said.

"Wind Cave is one of the most compact cave systems in the world. We've explored and mapped about one hundred fifty miles of caverns, but most of it is directly underneath us in a little more than a square mile of surface area."

"So, it goes down a long way."

"The deepest areas are about three hundred feet below the surface. That's not a long way down by geological measures."

Jill glared at me. "The Statue of Liberty is three hundred five feet high, and I remember that being a hell of a climb. I did that twenty years ago...and there were stairs."

Chris smiled at our interchange. "As I recall, Jill, you were one of the fittest rangers in the Ozarks. You could walk the legs off any of us. You look like you've kept yourself in shape."

"Okay, you've sweet talked me. Is Colleen nearby?"

Chris got up. "I think she's planning to guide one of the later tours. Let me see if she's around."

With Chris gone, Jill turned to me. "I don't like caves. I was offered a posting at Mammoth Cave National Park and I declined it. The thought of going into the cave, even once a week, was more than I was willing to contemplate."

Chris came back with a slender brown-haired ranger with a broad smile. "Jill and Doug Fletcher, this is Colleen O'Mara. She's my lead ranger in the caves. She's been here for five years and knows the cave network better than anyone. Jill and Doug are National Park Service investigators. Have a seat."

Colleen pulled a chair to the table. "How can I help you?"

"We're investigating the death of the guy who was found in the prairie." Jill explained. "He was seen in the campground with a woman, and she's disappeared. What are the chances she is lost in the cave?"

The question caught Colleen by surprise. "I don't think that's likely. We keep an eye on all the people on the tours and no one is missing. I mean, the tour groups aren't that big and the headcounts going in match the exit counts."

I leaned on the table. "There's a hole that was used to access the cave before the current entrance was opened. Could she have gone in there?"

"We don't use that as an access anymore. We just show that to people to demonstrate the air rushing in and out as the barometric pressure changes."

"But someone could get in there," I said.

"I guess someone *could* get in, but they'd have to crawl in on their hands and knees." Colleen paused. "Why would she do that?"

Jill replied with a question. "Have you ever been on a date that was so bad you wanted to sneak out the back door of a bar or restaurant? Imagine you'd maybe gotten drunk, returned with a guy to his trailer in a remote campground. You wake up and find out he's a total nutcase or he won't drive you back to civilization. Maybe he gets abusive and you panic and feel like you've got to escape. Or maybe you've taken something that makes you paranoid and you feel like you have to escape."

I could see that Colleen had lived that experience. She thought before answering. "There were still people around the campground then, so I'd probably have approached a female camper, or I'd have spoken to one of the rangers. I might've even walked out on the entrance road, hoping to hitchhike into town. I can't imagine a scenario where climbing into an unlit hole in the ground would seem like a better option than..." Colleen covered her mouth. "Shit, unless someone was chasing me, and I thought he was going to kill me."

Chris shook his head. "I'm having a hard time with this line of thought. The people in the campground and our hikers are like a fraternity of eco-friendly people. They smile, greet each other, offer to help if someone turns an ankle or needs water."

"Maybe I'm a jaded cop," I said, "but there are predators everywhere and national parks are not immune to them."

"Predator?" Chris asked.

"When I walked around St. Paul, I was taught to read faces. One out of a hundred had watchful eyes, looking for an opportunity to make a buck, exploit someone, or be a nuisance. There are another two or three percent who've

80

been victimized and their eyes are watchful, shying away from the predators and anything or anyone who looks threatening. Then, there's the rest of us, the sheep, who wander around unaware of the predators, trusting our fellow man, and unaware of the people who want to pick our pockets, break into our houses, steal our cars, or physically attack us. I think the people in the parks are mostly sheep, but there are predators, wolves, who slip in. That's why the National Park Service has law enforcement rangers who carry firearms and wear bullet-proof vests. More rangers are injured in attacks from humans than in falls and animal encounters combined."

Jill nodded. "And the proportions are shifting toward more human attacks."

Chris looked skeptically at Colleen. "How far would you have to go from the wind cave entrance to reach one of the main tour routes?"

"It's close to a mile and lots of it would be crawling on hands and knees."

"Can you find gear for Jill?"

Colleen sized up Jill. "Not a problem. I've got coveralls, helmets, lamps, gloves, and knee pads. Are you really willing to do this?"

The laser look I got from Jill could've melted steel. "Can we do it today or should we plan for tomorrow?"

"Give me fifteen minutes to change out of my uniform and into coveralls. Then, I'll pull out gear and be ready to go."

Jill smiled with her mouth, but not her eyes. "Great. Thank you."

Colleen left and Chris stood. "I doubt you're going to find anything, but you're in for quite an experience, Jill. There's nothing like spelunking with someone as experienced and interesting as Colleen."

"Gee, Doug, you'd better come along. It'll be a great bonding experience."

"Someone's got to interview the bartenders in Custer. I'll pick you up this afternoon."

Jill looked at Chris. "How long does it take to crawl a mile?"

Chris shook his head. "I don't know."

Chris left to check on tour coverage without Colleen.

Jill glared at me. "Colleen's changing into coveralls, so I assume that means we're going to get dirty. Buy a pair of pants for me while you're in Custer."

"What size?"

"You've been in my pants often enough; you should know the size."

"I specialized in panties, not jeans."

Jill closed her eyes. "Size six."

"What inseam?"

"Women's jeans don't have inseam lengths."

"I'll just buy a package of wet-wipes at a gas station so you can clean up."

That got me a withering glare. Jill was about to say something unkind, but Chris walked in. "That'll be just peachy. Thanks."

Chris smiled. "Peachy?"

Jill closed her eyes and bit her tongue. "Peachy. Fine. Flipping wonderful."

"Jill, you've cleaned up your language since the Ozarks. I recall your favorite adjective being something other than 'flipping.'"

I laughed. "She's reformed since our wedding. Her language is less salty now."

Colleen walked in on the end of the conversation carrying helmets, lanterns, and leather gloves. "Yes, please refrain from strong language. Spelunkers believe that swearing angers the underground trolls, so we tend to use drat, dang nabbit, golly, and other colorful, but less profane terms."

Jill accepted coveralls, a helmet, gloves, and knee pads. "Trolls? Really?"

Colleen smiled. "Caves are spooky places. Who's to say there aren't otherworldly beings roaming around in there. I prefer to err on the side of caution. Besides, I like to think I can come up with more adjectives than the F word. Also, Lakota legend believes their first people emerged from the windy hole, and I think swearing is in poor taste in a place that's revered as holy by the Native people."

"That I can accept. We should treat others' religious beliefs with reverence."

"Ready to go, Jill?"

Jill let out a sigh. "No point in delaying the inevitable." Jill accepted a helmet and lantern. She stopped at the doorframe and looked back at me. "If I die in the cave, promise you'll make a concerted effort to recover my body."

I looked at Chris, who was smiling. After she was gone Chris said, "Jill has always been a character. How did you get together?"

"Do you have an hour and a coffee pot?"

Chris waved me out the door and to an alcove off the visitor center. He grabbed two ceramic mugs from a drying rack, poured coffee, and led me back to his office. I closed the door as we walked in.

"Before I get into my history with Jill, are there any skeletons in her closet?"

Chris shook his head. "What happens in the park, stays in the park."

"Really? My experience has been that rangers are bigger gossips than cops, and that's a reach."

"Jill is about the straightest arrow I've ever worked with. She was serious about her job and wasn't into the stupid pranks and the hazing young rangers seem to delve into. Our bosses noticed her professionalism and that's why she moved up in the National Park Service while lots of our old associates moved to other endeavors."

"No miscues, reprimands, office romances?"

Chris leaned back. "You sound like you're doing a background check for a job opening."

"My life was a mess. I was a divorced drunk who was trying to hit the reset button on my life when I met Jill. She hired me to investigate a murder, treated me professionally, and supported every decision I made. I updated her every night on the progress of my investigation, and after a while, those conversations felt more like friendship than boss and employee. I was moving to Padre Island National Seashore, and I invited her along to see if there was a spark between us. She agreed to give it a try and we fell in love."

"That's a touching story. So why are you trying to find out about her past?"

"Like I said, I was a mess, and I sometimes struggle with her acceptance of my checkered past. I feel like the luckiest guy in the world and I'm still trying to figure out how she's willing to put up with a cynical old cop who's battered in both body and mind."

Chris glanced at the door. "Every young male ranger tried to date Jill. She was classy and polished. She saw through their efforts to cultivate romance. She'd seen enough of them bedding a pretty young thing, then putting a notch in their pistols before moving to another conquest. I think you found the key to Jill's heart—you were the friend she needed." Chris took a sip of coffee and smiled. "Jill's a very special person. You may be one of the luckiest guys in the world."

"You're married?"

"I married a nice girl from the Ozarks, and she's followed me from park to park. We have three grown kids, and Custer will be home until I retire. I expect we'll move to Rapid City to be closer to our grandchildren, but we'll stay in the Black Hills."

"That's what Jess Pond said, too. He plans to retire here at the end of his FBI career."

"It's a nice place, Doug. The people are friendly. It's pretty. There's no state income tax. Housing is affordable. I don't know about you, but I'd have a real problem moving to Denver or Minneapolis, much less L.A., New York or Washington D.C."

Chris answered the knock on his door and a red-haired, freckled guy stuck his head in. "Excuse me, Chris, but I'm ready to make a loop around the park, and you wanted me to meet the investigators."

Chris waved the young ranger into his office. "Paul, this is Doug Fletcher. His wife, Jill, went with Colleen to check out the original entrance. Paul is the one who discovered the hiker's body."

We shook hands. "Like I said, I'm ready to make a loop of the park. Would you like to ride along, Mr. Fletcher?"

"You can ride with Paul, or if you need to go into Custer, you two can spend time together this afternoon or tomorrow."

I grabbed my coat. "I'd like to see where you found the hiker before the snowstorm hits."

"I can get close, but if you want to see the actual spot where we recovered the body, we'll have to hike a couple miles."

"Let's start out driving to the area and see where to go from there." I stepped to the door. "If Jill beats me back, let her know where I am."

Chris shook his head. "Jill's not going to beat you back. I'll bet on that."

Chapter Six

Paul's pickup was idling outside the visitor center. The windows had melted clear and it was warm inside. I peeled off my coat and set it on the back seat. "Have you been at Wind Cave a long time, Paul?"

"It'll be two years in May. I got hired when I graduated from the South Dakota School of Mines and Technology."

"Where's that campus?"

"SDSM&T is in Rapid City."

"Is the Black Hills home?"

"No, I grew up in Redfield, in the middle of the state. Moving to Rapid City for college was coming to the big city. Chris said you're a National Park Service investigator from Texas here to look into the death of the hiker we found."

"Yes, I got a call last week asking if we could fly up here to look at your suspicious hiker death."

"You willingly left Texas to fly to South Dakota in December. You must be crazy or very dedicated."

"My wife, Jill, is from Spearfish and this gives us a chance to spend Christmas with her family, so it was convenient. Tell me how you discovered the dead hiker."

"I make this circuit every day, and I know the terrain and the animals. The animals migrate with the seasons, and I can kind of predict where they're going to be. There's not much around where the body was except prairie dogs and coyotes this time of year. I was surprised to see magpies and crows hanging around, so I thought something pretty big had died because they don't gather around a dead mouse cr prairie dog. So, I watched them for a bit, then parked and hiked out to see what had died. I thought it might have been one of the tagged buffalo that had been sick and wandered off. Then I saw a golden eagle picking on a carcass. The eagle flew off when I approached and there he was."

"Tell me about the body."

"It was bad. I mean the guy's face was gone. Other than that, it just looked like he might've lay down and fallen asleep. I thought he'd probably gotten disoriented while hiking and died of hypothermia. He was a long way from anything."

"How was he dressed?"

"Blue North Face ski jacket, jeans, hiking boots. There was a backpack next to him like he'd just taken it off and set it on the ground."

"Blood?"

"His face and neck were a bloody mess."

"Was there blood on his clothes, on the ground, sprayed on the grass around him?"

Paul glanced at me. "He didn't die of hypothermia?"

"I spoke with the forensic pathologist. He died of blood loss."

Paul thought about the revelation for a moment. "I'm sorry, sir. I didn't notice any blood other than on his face and neck. It had snowed and thawed a couple times in the previous week and if there was any blood spread around, I didn't notice it."

"Did you see anything else unusual in the days and weeks before you found the body?"

"Unusual? Like what?"

"Strange people. People acting like they didn't belong here or weren't dressed for camping and hiking?"

"You think someone killed him?"

"That's a possibility. Can you think of some other reason he would've bled to death in the middle of nowhere?"

"This is...crazy. I mean, no one murders someone out here." Paul thought. "If I had to speculate, and I'm just talking as I'm thinking, I'd guess that he irritated a buffalo. They're inquisitive and sometimes walk up to people to see what they're doing."

"Were there buffalo in the area?"

"Not usually, but they move around."

"How would someone look if they'd been killed in a buffalo encounter?"

"I don't know. I suppose they'd be stomped or gored somehow."

90

"You said he was just laying on the ground next to his backpack. He didn't have any broken bones or contusions anywhere but his neck. Do you think that sounds like a buffalo encounter?"

Paul shook his head. "I think anyone attacked by a buffalo would be pretty battered."

"Do you have any other thoughts?"

Paul thought as we drove. "Suicide. I mean, he was just sitting there, kind of serenely. Maybe he overdosed and the carrion feeders found the body when he started to decompose."

"He bled to death. It wasn't an overdose."

"I don't know. Maybe he slit his wrists?"

"The carotid artery in his neck was slit. I've never heard of anyone cutting their own neck to commit suicide."

Paul digested that and was silent. We stopped at a small rise and he pointed toward an area of prairie below us. It was pockmarked with brown splotches, and prairie dogs started popping up on those spots more than a mile from the road we were on.

Paul rolled down his window. "Can you hear them whistling? They see us, but we're so far away they're not spooked, just curious. If we walk closer, they'll sound an alarm and will all scramble down their holes."

"That's where you found the body?"

Paul nodded. "It was like he was sitting there watching the prairie dog town, then just laid back and died." Paul pointed to an area on the far side of the prairie dog town.

"Can we drive over there?"

Paul shook his head. "I can't drive the truck across the prairie. If people see tire tracks off the road, they'll think they can drive all over the park. We could walk over there."

I reached for my coat. "Sure. Let's take a walk."

Paul moved like my old partner, Jamie, who was a Navajo Nation policeman. He glided across the ground while I stumbled on the uneven terrain, tripping over rocks hidden under the snow and getting my boots tangled in sagebrush clumps. I was breathing heavily and was sweaty despite the searing cold that numbed my nose. We'd walked over half an hour when Paul stopped on the edge of the prairie dog town.

"This is the spot?" I asked.

"Yeah, generally." He looked around. "It's kind of hard to pinpoint the exact spot. The terrain looks much the same all around here, and we didn't put up a flag or anything."

"What kind of predators hang around here?"

"Badgers sometimes get into the prairie dog towns and dig after them. We reintroduced black-footed ferrets a few years ago, and their primary food source is the prairie dogs."

"I'm thinking something that's big enough to rip open a man's throat."

Paul looked at me, studying my face to see if I was kidding. "I suppose a cougar is capable of doing that. They're sometimes aggressive toward people. There are a few black bears, but they're shy and tend to run from human encounters. Bobcats are small and wouldn't attack a human. There are coyotes, but they're after rabbits, mice, and small animals, not humans. There've been a couple gray wolf sightings in Custer State Park, just west of here. It's possible a wolf could've wandered through, but there hasn't been a wolf pack in the Black Hills in over a hundred years. Besides, no one's ever reported a wolf attack on a human outside of Alaska."

I looked at the landscape. "If the victim died, who'd report an attack?"

"Let's say in modern times anyway. Predator attacks aren't tidy and rescue teams are dispatched when people are missing. Even a grizzly bear attack leaves a lot of...evidence behind. Predators aren't tidy."

"Could a wolf rip open a man's throat?"

"The wolf attack videos I've seen show them taking out a moose or deer's legs, then clamping their jaws on the prey's throat until they suffocate. They don't rip throats open."

"Badgers?"

"Nah. They'll burrow away unless you corner them."

"Wolverines? Lynx? Grizzly Bears?"

"They were all probably here at some point in history, but I doubt any of them have been seen in the Black Hills for over a hundred years. They're not very compatible with civilization."

"That leaves us with a cougar," I said.

Paul nodded. "I've heard of cougar attacks in California and Arizona. But they seem to be chasing someone who's running, like a predatory response of to fleeing prey animal. This guy looks like he was just sitting there."

I'd cooled off, and my sweat was starting to chill me. "Let's walk back."

I stumbled along behind Paul, and he took long strides, avoiding the sagebrush clumps and somehow missing the rocks hidden under the snow. I was sweaty again when we got to the truck, so I threw my coat in the backseat.

"Okay, Paul, so let's assume this guy was attacked by a cougar while he was sitting there. The cougar sneaks up behind him, takes a swipe at his neck and he bleeds out. Then the cougar just wanders off until the crows and magpies find him. Does that sound like a possible scenario?"

Paul shook his head. "I read about a cougar attack in Arizona last year. A mother took down a hiker, dragged him away from the trail, then she and her two cubs were eating the carcass until other hikers reported it."

"If a cougar had attacked the hiker, it would've been for food. It wouldn't have been just an attack to kill him then leave his body?"

"I think a cougar would've dragged his body somewhere it would've kept it out of sight from coyotes and wolves unless there was something that chased it off before it could eat…him." Paul stared out the windshield.

"Cougars eat deer and smaller prey. I just don't see that happening."

"We're back to a human attack."

Paul closed his eyes. "Our campers are friendly and easy-going. Hikers greet and help each other. They don't kill one another."

"Do you walk the campground?"

"Not regularly, but yeah, sometimes."

"Do you ever see someone who makes you just a little uneasy? You know, someone who seems to avoid eye contact or acts like they're hiding something?"

"Once in a while. It's usually some college-aged kids who're smoking marijuana. I smell the marijuana before I see them."

"You've never seen indigents in the campground who look like they're just going from campground to campground, maybe someone who might check out the neighboring campsites when no one's watching."

Paul looked uncomfortable. "We get some folks who look like they're having a tough go of it. I wouldn't characterize them as thieves, more as hippies. I don't see those folks killing someone. They've made a life choice different from the people who show up in fancy clothes, new boots, and RVs the size of a Greyhound bus with an air conditioner on top."

"You don't approve of the big RV people?"

"I'm more of a minimalist. I'd rather sleep in a two-man tent with all my belongings in a backpack."

"Take nothing but pictures. Leave nothing but footprints."

"That too but to leave no carbon footprint. I've got teams of volunteers who come in every spring and summer to pick invasive species in the prairie. You know, to bring the prairie back to native plants."

"Someone took the dead hiker's pickup, and a guy has been using his cash card at a Rapid City ATM." Paul put the truck in gear, and we drove in silence for twenty minutes. "You got quiet, Paul."

He glanced at me. "Mr. Fletcher…"

"Call me Doug, please."

"Okay, Doug, I don't want to think about the possible scenarios that would involve someone killing a camper and stealing his stuff. I'd like to believe that kind of thing doesn't happen in a national park."

I smiled. "It usually doesn't, but then something like this comes up. That's why I've got a job and why I carry a weapon. When I'm patrolling in Texas, I wear a bullet-proof vest."

"Really?"

"More rangers are injured and killed by visitors than animal attacks and falls. And there's an internet site dedicated to the investigation of the dozens of people who've disappeared from National Parks in the past forty years."

Paul considered that in silence until we parked at the visitor center. "I wish I could say this has been a pleasure but hanging around you is a real downer."

I shook his hand. "Paul, most of the National Park Service interactions are pleasant and upbeat. Our visitors are mostly happy people who come here to be refreshed and learn. They want to meet upbeat, enthusiastic rangers like you."

"But the National Park Service needs people like you, too."

"I'm afraid so."

We walked into the visitor center and found Chris in his office. I shook Paul's hand again. "Thanks for the tour."

Paul forced a smile. "I wish I could say it's been a pleasure." He left me with Chris.

"I don't suppose Jill and Colleen are back."

Chris looked at his watch. "I think we've got time to go into Custer for lunch." He pulled a coat off a peg behind his office door. "I'll drive."

We were on the drive to Custer when Chris spoke up. "How was your drive with Paul?"

"We went out to where the body was found and walked out to the prairie dog town. It's a long way from anything. We talked about animal attacks and the probability that the attack was human. Paul was uncomfortable with that."

"That's the background on his strange parting comment?"

"I was a bit of a downer for him. He's a good ranger and looks at the good side of people. I opened the book on the dark side, and he wasn't at…a teachable moment."

"We hire a lot of people with deep environmental views on the park and what we represent. You're digging at the dark underbelly I'm sure they'd like to ignore."

"You hire hippies and I'm a cynical cop. Is that what you're telling me?"

"I wouldn't call my rangers hippies. They're committed to protecting the park resources, and that's a good thing. They may be a little naïve about the darker side of life. How long were you a cop?"

"I spent twenty years with the St. Paul police."

"I imagine you saw every seedy distasteful thing there is to experience."

"Let's not get into details, but there are people out there who are willing to do unthinkable things to others."

"People with personality disorders that allow them to act without remorse?"

I thought for a minute. "I guess that's probably a good characterization of a lot of criminals. I have a hard time separating the people who get 'hospitalized' for mental defects that allowed them to kill someone from the person who goes to prison for the same crime."

"One doesn't understand his crime versus one who knows he's doing something wrong but does it anyway."

Chris pulled up in front of a place with a sign that said it was a saloon. "We're drinking our lunch?" I asked.

"This place has the best burgers in town, and you said you wanted to show our victim's picture to the Custer bartenders. We can kill two birds with one stone."

The saloon's interior was knotty pine, and the walls were covered with bear skins and mounted deer, buffalo, and antelope heads. There was a full body taxidermy mount of a whitetail buck on a shelf over the front door. Chris picked a high-top table near the back, and I took a seat facing the front door.

A middle-aged waitress with a big smile walked over with menus. "Hey, Chris, I haven't seen you in here recently."

"Hi, Rhonda. Bitsy and I usually come in for supper after you're off. This is my friend, Doug. Treat him right. He's a ranger."

Rhonda laughed. "Like we treat the rangers any different than anyone else. What would you like to drink?"

We ordered diet Cokes and Rhonda left us with the menus. I glanced through the options, which seemed to be average café fare. "Anything special I should get or avoid?"

"I like the bison burger because it's a little leaner than the beef, but everything is good."

Rhonda came back with our drinks. "What did you decide on?"

Chris ordered the bison burger basket, and I ordered a California burger. I pulled out my phone and pulled up Palmer's picture. "Did you see this guy in here last week?"

Rhonda took my phone and studied the picture. "This picture is terrible. Is it from a mug shot or a driver's license?"

"It's a driver's license photo."

"He might've had a couple days growth of beard if he was here," Chris added.

"I don't recognize him. Can I show this to Waldo, the bartender?"

"Sure. He might've been in here with a woman."

Chris leaned close. "What are the odds that he was here?"

"Probably pretty small, but that's how police work goes. You ask a lot of questions and show pictures to a lot of people to get that one nugget that cracks the case."

Rhonda returned with my phone. "Waldo doesn't remember him either. How long ago do you think he was here?"

I took my phone and shut it down. "Probably last week."

"Sorry, but we don't remember him."

"Jill told me to buy her jeans. Is there a clothing store in town?"

"Yeah, Flora's is across the street and a block down. She's got western-style clothes. If Jill's an off the rack size, you should find something as long as she doesn't mind bootcut jeans."

"Chances are whatever I buy will be wrong, but let's try Flora's."

Our burgers arrived, and we made small talk about the National Park Service, rural South Dakota, and Custer. I told Chris about being tested by my father-in-law and he laughed. I paid for lunch, and we walked outside into the sunshine and wind with a bite.

"Flora's is this way. There are a couple more restaurants and bars along the way if you want to show the picture around town."

We stopped at a sports-themed bar, with televisions broadcasting football and basketball. Neither of the two waitresses nor the bartender recognized Steve Palmer's picture. We had the same result at another western-themed bar across the street from Flora's.

A pleasant, middle-aged woman with her hair tied in a ponytail was working behind the counter at Flora's. "How can I help you?"

"I need a pair of size six women's jeans."

"Would you like Lee, Levi's, or Wrangler?" I looked lost. "How tall is your wife and is she trim or average?"

"She's slender, although she hates to hear people say that, and she's five-eight."

"I think you should try Levi's," the clerk said, leading me down an aisle lined with women's shirts, jeans, and belts. "Which style does she prefer?"

"Style?"

"Button-fly, zipper-fly, boot-cut, taper-cut, low-rise or regular waist?"

I closed my eyes trying to visualize Jill in jeans. "Zipper. Regular waist. Boot cut. Anything else?"

"Dark blue, acid-washed, or stone-washed?"

I threw my head back. "Plain old denim blue."

The clerk smiled and offered her hand. "I'm Flora, and today I'm going to save your butt. She selected a pair of jeans from a shelf. "How long have you been married to this woman?"

"A little over six months."

I followed her to the cash register and had my charge card in hand. "Is there anything else? Maybe something for Christmas?"

I looked at Chris who was grinning. "My shopping is done, Doug. How about you?"

"Jill's best friend, Mandy, delivered a wrapped present in a small box and told me it was my gift to Jill, but I haven't purchased anything for her."

"Doug, as a man who's been married a long time, let me give you some advice. This is your first Christmas together. She expects something under the tree that you purchased. It doesn't have to be expensive or fancy, but it's got to be something you bought, and it has to appear you gave it some thought."

"You're saying not a gift card."

Flora laughed. "You really haven't been married long, have you. C'mon with me." She led me to a counter filled with turquoise and gold jewelry. "Does she wear jewelry?"

"Just little earrings."

"Are her ears pierced?"

I closed my eyes and Flora laughed again. "Yes, they're pierced."

"These are Black Hills gold. They've got trace metals that give them pink and green hues."

I looked at Chris, who was nodding. "I'll take them."

Flora closed the counter and wrapped the earring box in Christmas paper. She handed it to me and pointed to a rack of western cut women's blouses. "She's size six pants. Is she buxom, so she wears a larger size blouse?"

"She's more of a tomboy who wears sports bras."

Flora pulled three blouses off the rack, each with a different shade of plaid. "These are medium, which sounds like your best bet. It's off-season so they're on clearance."

Chris leaned close. "Take all three."

I nodded. "Can you Christmas wrap them too?"

"Of course!"

After half an hour in the store, I'd managed to add triple digits to my charge card balance and had a bag full of clothing, most intended as Christmas presents in sizes and styles I hoped would fit and match Jill's tastes.

I was ready to walk out, then stopped and opened my phone. "Have you seen this guy? He might've been here about a week or ten days ago."

Flora looked at the picture and shook her head.

"He might've had a couple-day-old beard and been with a woman."

She considered the picture again and I saw recognition in her eyes. "Sure. The woman was shopping in here, and he came in when she was checking out."

I looked around the ceiling. "Do you have security video of them?"

"There's not much call for it around here. Not a lot of shoplifting."

"Describe the woman."

"She was kind of average height, maybe five-six. Her hair was blonde, but it was kind of frosted, like young women do, with darker roots."

"How old was she?"

"I'd guess about nineteen or twenty. If I'd been working at the bar, I would've asked to see her ID."

"She wasn't someone you recognized from town?"

"She wasn't local. She struck me as more of a college student, with jeans with holes in them, not from wear, but from the store." The woman's eyes lit up. "She was wearing a BHSU hoodie."

I looked at Chris. "What's BHSU?"

"Black Hills State University. It's in Rapid City."

I turned to Flora. "Did you notice anything about them as a couple?"

"What do you mean?"

"Were they friendly, angry, acting like lovebirds?"

Flora cocked her head. "He seemed...impatient. She'd been shopping for like forty-five minutes, trying on clothes and boots. She'd set a couple things on the counter but was looking at shirts. His body language said he was ready to go, and she was still thinking about some purchases. He kind of herded her to the counter and she checked out before she was ready to go. I think she was kind of...maybe bullied by him. I don't know. If I had to guess, they weren't in a balanced relationship. He was in charge, and she was going along with it. If I'd known them, I'd say they were in an abusive relationship or on the verge of a breakup."

I was getting excited. "But they bought something?"

"Yes, the girl had a pair of jeans and a cheap necklace."

"Who paid and did they use a credit card?"

"She paid. I remember it because her credit card was refused, so she got all flustered and switched to a debit card."

I almost pumped my hand in the air. "Can I see a copy of the receipt?"

The clerk looked at me skeptically. "We don't give out customer information."

I opened my coat so she could see my badge and I pulled out my ID and showed it to her.

"National Park Service?"

"I'm a National Park Service investigator and this woman has been missing for a week. We've been trying to find her. The guy you identified died in Wind Cave park shortly after they were here."

"It'll take me a second, but I can pull it up on the computer." Flora typed into the computer, then spun the screen so I could see it. The signature was indecipherable, but the name on the card was Brigette Daly.

"Can you print that for me?"

Flora smiled. "Sure, but only because you've been such a good customer."

* * *

I called Jess Pond from the pickup on our drive back to the park. "I've got a possible ID on the woman who was with our victim. She made a charge on a debit card in Custer with the name Brigette Daly. She was wearing a BHSU hoodie at the time of the purchase."

"I'll get someone over to BHSU right away to see if she's missing, or better yet, still around with knowledge of what happened to our victim."

I ended the call and Chris smiled. "Is that a big break in the case?"

"It's sure a milestone. If Brigette is on campus, we may be able to break this open. If they haven't seen her recently, it may lead us to another whole investigation."

Chapter Seven

Jill and Colleen were standing in the visitor center looking like they'd been rolling in dirt.

Jill's initial glare softened when I held up the pair of new jeans. "Did you find anything?"

"Dirt, bats, and bat guano," she replied as she sped by, handing me her filthy jacket, and snatching the jeans from my hand.

Colleen watched Jill duck into the women's restroom. "She's a trouper, Doug. We were on our hands and knees, our bellies, and sliding along like snakes. Jill never complained or made a derisive comment. I think you should keep her around."

I smiled. "Jill told you we are newlyweds?"

"We got through a lot of topics crawling around down there. I even know what you're getting for Christmas." Colleen paused. "Excuse me. I'm going to change back into my clean uniform."

Chris led me back to his office where I set Jill's dirty jacket on the floor. "So, Doug, what's next?"

"I'd like a list of the people registered in the campground while our victim was there. I hope one of them has a cellphone photo or video with our victim and the woman in the background. I'd also like to do background checks on the campers. Somebody stole the truck out of the campground along with the victim's wallet and ID."

"We don't control access to the park or the campground, so anyone could've driven in and taken the truck."

"Not without an accomplice. A second person had to drive the stolen truck away."

Jill walked into Chris's office just as my cellphone buzzed. "Fletcher."

"Doug, this is Jess. There's no one named Brigette Daly registered at BHSU. There is a woman by that name who lives in Sturgis. I tracked her down, and she knows nothing about her card being used in Custer. She checked her purse while I had her on the phone, and she confirmed that the card was in her possession. I've been going back and forth with her and the bank and there were a number of transactions she didn't make on the card. The bank is sending me a list of the bogus transactions, and I'll call the businesses to see if any of them have security footage of the person using the card."

"How can someone have their card in their hand, yet have someone making purchases with it?"

"Well, there are a couple options. She may have used it at a gas pump or ATM that had a card skimmer picking the numbers off the cards people were running, then transmitting the card information to a remote location. Or a waitress or hostess may have recorded the number when they ran it for a charge at a restaurant. The criminals take the card information and make a duplicate or just start making internet purchases with the number."

"Life used to be simpler when we all used cash."

Jill leaned close to the phone. "Hi, Jess, this is Jill. Ignore Doug, he's a dinosaur."

Jess laughed. "Yeah, we'd all like to go back to simpler times. These cybercrimes are just eating up my agents' time and the criminals are getting more and more sophisticated. It's driving us nuts. Give me a good old bank robbery and let me track down the car and driver."

"Jess, I think Jill and I will hit the rest of the stores and restaurants in Custer this afternoon to see if any of them have video of the woman. Tomorrow we'll check Keystone."

"I thought you guys were going to check Wind Cave to see if the woman got lost inside the cave."

Jill grabbed the phone. "Doug bailed, but I crawled through the original opening with one of the rangers this morning. We didn't find anything. Now Doug is going to take me out to eat, then we're going back to Spearfish so I can scrub some cave grime off my skin."

"How much of the cave did you check?"

"Colleen said we got through about a mile of the difficult entrance, then we walked up the part of the area open to tours. They keep track of the headcount on tours real closely, so we thought that if the woman had been in the cave she would've crawled in through the original opening. There was no sign anyone had been in that area for a long time. The dirt floor was undisturbed, and we slid through some holes that would've been daunting without helmets and good lights."

"They're one hundred percent sure the woman didn't wander away from a tour group?" Jess asked.

I pushed the phone in front of the superintendent. "Hi, Jess. This is Chris Ostberg. There is virtually no way for someone to walk away from a tour group unnoticed. The rangers guide relatively small groups which they keep close together, and they do a headcount going in and going out. There's no way someone slipped away without being noticed."

"And there's no way for someone to get in other than with a ranger or through the entrance Jill took?"

"We control access and limit the entry to guided groups. The visitor center is locked when we leave so no one can get in after we close down."

"There's no chance she could've hidden in a bathroom and slipped out after you locked up?"

Chris closed his eyes. "Jess, there's a very remote possibility something like that could happen. We shut off the bathroom lights and walk through before we leave, but we don't check every bathroom stall to make sure there's no one hiding from us."

"Chris, is there any way someone who was determined to get past you could've accessed the cave after you closed up?"

Chris sighed. "If someone were very determined and devious, I suppose it's possible they'd be in the visitor center, but we shut down the elevator so there's no other way to access the cave."

Jill leaned close to the phone. "I suggested to Colleen that the woman might've been desperate to escape from the victim or was on a 'bad trip' and was extremely paranoid after taking some drug. In a worst case, she might've been desperate to try anything to escape. Colleen countered that there are uniformed rangers around, particularly in the visitor center, and someone in trouble could've approached any of them to seek protection."

There was a pause before Jess responded. "I've got three agents chasing needles in a haystack all over western South Dakota trying to track down a man who used the victim's ATM card, and now we're trying to follow up on a card that was apparently skimmed off a card reader somewhere. None of those leads are any more substantial than the chance the unidentified woman slipped by the rangers and hid in the cave."

Jess let that dangle until Chris responded. "I get it, Jess. I'll have people geared up and searching areas off the tour routes first thing in the morning."

I shut down the phone and looked at Chris and Jill. "Well, I guess it's only fair that the National Park Service should be putting out as much effort as the FBI to solve our mystery."

Chris shook his head. "We're talking a needle in a haystack. If this woman did get past us, she was very determined, and I can't see a scenario where anyone would go deep into a dark cave to hide and not be seen by my rangers." He paused. "But, hey, I'll make sure we put in a good effort."

Jill looked anxious. "You don't need us to help, do you?"

"You guys have other leads to follow. I'll pull together everyone I can break loose from other duties and I'll go in myself. I should be able to get three teams going."

"Will you be able to search the whole cave?" I asked.

"Like I said, there's one hundred fifty miles of cave," Chris explained. "So, no, we won't be able to get to all of it in a day."

"But you'll be able to check for footprints, so you'll know if someone went through a particular passage?"

Chris shook his head. "There's no wind or water erosion in the cave, so it's impossible to determine of a footprint is an hour or a hundred years old."

Jill perked up. "But most of your rangers are men, and they could look for a woman's small footprints."

Chris smiled. "Collen's been on nearly all the recent explorations."

"Collen's boots are distinctive and she's probably the only woman who's been off the guided trails any time recently," Jill noted. "Our lost woman was probably in athletic shoes rather than boots."

"That's an interesting point. I'll pass that along to the search teams."

I stood up. "Sounds like a plan. Jill and I will show the victim's photo around Custer and Keystone. Jess's agents are following up on the places Brigette Daly's card was used. Maybe between the three approaches we'll come up with something."

Jill carried her filthy jacket to the front door and stopped. "Warm up the pickup. I don't want to get the seat dirty, so I'll run out and throw my coat in the back seat."

"It's a National Park Service pickup. It's had dirt on the seats before."

Jill glared at me. "I'm the one who would be sitting in that dirt tomorrow, unless you want to let me drive tomorrow and you can sit in the dirty seat."

I pulled out the keys and went out the door to warm up the truck.

* * *

I took off my coat and put it in the backseat and Jill ran from the visitor center to the truck. She put her coat on the backseat floor and got in the passenger seat.

"What's in the shopping bag?"

"It's a little close to Christmas to be asking questions like that."

Jill smiled. Her dimples always melted my heart. "You bought me a Christmas present in Custer?"

"I'm not playing twenty questions."

She leaned over and kissed my cheek. "That's sweet, but where is there any shopping in Custer? The Shopko store went out of business and lots of the tourist places close in the winter."

"Like I said, it's too close to Christmas to be asking questions."

Jill settled in, staring at me, while trying to envision a shopping place in Custer.

I decided to change the topic. "How do your jeans fit?"

"They're a little loose, but they shrink a bit in the dryer. They should be perfect." Her eyes lit up and she smiled. "You found a Christmas present in the western store?"

"I said…"

"Yeah, yeah. 'It's too close to Christmas.' Let's see. What else does the western store carry? You don't know my shoe size, so you didn't get boots."

"Just quit there and leave it be."

"We haven't spent Christmas together, so you don't know the lengths I went to in my search for presents when I was a kid. I'd check the wastebasket for store receipts. I knew where every box was hidden, and I'd shaken them all. I'd peel back the corner of wrapping paper to look at the boxes to see which store the presents came from."

She leaned back and lifted my coat off the shopping bag. "You shopped at Flora's. Yup, western wear. I bet you picked up some great closeout deals. Let's see. Jeans? Shirts? Belts? Boots?"

"Geez, will you let it go? You're not eight years old anymore."

I glanced at her, and her eyes were twinkling. "Doug, Christmas is one of the times when the little kid in me comes out. Revel in it."

She reached over the seat and fingered the boxes. "These are the size of clothing boxes. I'm guessing you got me some western shirts."

"Actually, Chris and I drove into Rapid City and shopped at Victoria's Secret. Chris gave me a bag from Flora's."

"There's no way you had time to drive to Rapid City and back. You went to Flora's."

We went back and forth until we got to Custer. "I'm starving. Stop at the café."

I parked on the street directly in front of the café. It was off season and mid-afternoon and there was no competition for parking spots. The café was empty, and the only waitress was filling sugar containers. She brought menus with a smile. "What can I get you to drink?"

"Black coffee," I replied.

"Same for me. What's your soup?"

"We've got chili and there might be one bowl of chicken wild rice left."

Jill handed the waitress her menu. "Chili sounds great."

I gave her my menu. "I'll just have coffee, thanks."

"Was the cave spooky?"

"Not spooky, just claustrophobic. I did pretty well until we got in some really tight places, then I was paranoid about getting separated from Colleen. She knew I was a novice, so she didn't let me out of sight."

The waitress brought our coffee. I pulled out my phone. "Have you seen this guy? He might've been around about a week ago with a young woman."

The waitress, whose nametag said, 'Alice' looked at the photo and shook her head. "I don't recall him being around."

"He might've had a couple day's growth of beard and the girl was wearing a BHSU hoodie."

Alice studied the photo. "I don't think so, but I've seen a lot of folks since last week. Unless they stirred up trouble or left a million-dollar tip, I probably wouldn't remember them." She handed the phone back. "Why are you asking?"

"The guy died in the park last week and the girl is missing."

Alice's eyes drifted to the badge on my belt. "You guys are rangers?"

"We're National Park Service investigators."

"My husband is a Custer County deputy sheriff. Have you been over to the sheriff's office and asked them about this guy and girl?"

"No, we haven't done that yet."

"Can I use your phone?"

"Sure," I said.

Alice entered a number and waited. "Hey, Butch, there are a couple of National Park Service investigators here eating lunch and they're asking about the guy who died out at Wind Cave. Can you swing by?"

She ended the call and handed the phone back to me. "He's over at the courthouse, shouldn't take him but five minutes to get here."

Alice brought a bowl that must've held a quart of chili. It was covered with diced raw onions and had a dollop of sour cream on top of it. Jill appraised it and asked for a second spoon.

She slid the bowl between us. "You'd better have some just so we have the same onion breath."

We were about halfway through the chili when a deputy walked in and waved. He nodded to Alice who immediately poured a mug of coffee and delivered it before he was seated.

"Butch Henry," he said as he shook my hand.

"Doug and Jill Fletcher."

He nodded thanks to Alice. He looked at my badge, and I slid out my credentials and passed them to him.

He looked at them and set them on the table next to me. "I've met some law enforcement rangers, but I've never met a National Park Service investigator before. Someone must be very concerned about this dead guy."

"There's a dead guy and a missing girl. On top of that, someone took the dead guy's pickup, abandoned it in Rapid City, and used his debit card in an ATM by the university."

Butch considered that. "Well, to use his card in an ATM means the dead guy must've given him his PIN. That implies they were really good buddies, or the dead guy gave it up under duress before he died."

I took out my phone and pulled up the picture of the victim. "Here's the dead guy. His name is Steve Palmer. The woman was with him at Flora's last week wearing a BHSU hoodie and using a credit card that was apparently skimmed off an ATM or gas pump. The FBI spoke with the credit card holder, and she had the card in her possession and was unaware the number was being used."

Butch looked at the picture and handed it back. "Is the guy a local?"

"He's from Mitchell and was camping at Wind Cave. He was alone when he showed up, then the woman was with him a day later. I've been showing his picture around hoping we could find out where he picked up the woman."

"Your theory is that he picked her up in a bar and you're hoping they have surveillance video of the two of them."

"Exactly. We know they were in Custer together, so we were going to show his picture around town and then hit the bars in Keystone."

"Email that picture to me. If things stay slow, I can hit some of the bars in the evening and maybe check some motels, stores and other places."

I sent him the picture. "The girl is young. The clerk at Flora's said if she'd been a bartender, she would've carded her. She has frosted blonde hair with dark underneath, and the BHSU hoodie."

"I suppose the girl might be, or have been a BHSU student, but those shirts are all over. She could've got it from a boyfriend or bought it at a garage sale or thrift shop. It's hard to pin that down."

Jill pushed her chili aside with a quarter of it still in the bowl. "We're concerned that Palmer and the girl had a falling out and she may be dead, injured, or on the run."

Butch nodded. "Maybe she was the bait in a trap and her accomplice used her to get your dead guy's ATM card, PIN, and helped him steal the pickup."

"Sure," I said. "We've been assuming she was a victim, but we know she used a phony card at Flora's. It would make sense that she's somehow involved in a scam."

Jill let out a sigh. "And the BHSU hoodie would be perfect for helping set her up as a drunk coed who was looking for a party and agreed to go back to the guy's campground."

Butch signaled for a coffee refill. "We've had some women working the motels and campgrounds. She might be a prostitute and the guy using the dead guy's card in the ATM is her pimp or boyfriend."

Jill closed her eyes. "I'm from Spearfish and I'd like to believe that kind of thing doesn't happen around here."

Butch smiled. "There've been working girls here since the gold rush days, and I think there's been a resurgence since Deadwood opened the casinos. And don't even get me started on the 'tent bunnies' who hop between campsites during Sturgis bike week."

"I suppose there's all kinds of vices that arrive with the bikers," I said.

Butch shook his head. "They're always here but there's certainly an influx of all kinds of crime. We've made drug busts, broken up fights, arrested hookers, and more. Hell, we detained a woman at a motel after the management complained about a loud party. She was entertaining a roomful of drunk guys. She had a thousand dollars in her bag and a duffle bag full of cash in her car."

Alice had been topping off our coffee and overheard the conversation. "It's a lot easier to make a fistful of cash on your back than it is waiting tables."

We thanked Butch, paid Alice for the chili and coffee along with a generous tip.

Jill scampered to the pickup and snuggled up close while we waited for the heater. "What's your cop gut saying to you about this woman?"

"Something I learned from an old detective was incredibly wise. He told me to follow the evidence and not make the evidence fit what you believe."

"Yeah, but you've told me you follow your nose. Where's your nose telling you to go?"

"My nose is telling me to take you to a shower because you've been crawling in bat shit."

Jill sniffed the air. "I don't smell anything."

"That's because it's you who stinks." I put the truck into gear and drove north while Jill buckled her seatbelt.

"I thought we were going to stop places and show the picture around."

"The more you warm up the gamier you get. I think any respectable place would throw you out."

"Alice didn't say anything."

"We were the only people in the place. She's probably got a bucket of bleach and is wiping down the table, chairs, and the floor where you'd rested your feet."

Jill reached over the seat for the bag in the back seat. "Do you have a pair of shoes in the shopping bag?"

"I told you…"

"I need to get out of more than these jeans if I really smell that bad. My parents picked up your mom at the airport this afternoon, and I don't want to show up at the house smelling like a manure pit."

"You're not using this as an excuse to open your Christmas presents early."

Jill pulled the bag into the front seat. "Presents as in plural?"

I put my hand on the bag. "Listen to me. You're not opening anything in the bag today. Period."

She got a sly grin. "Maybe just one. You said there are several." She sniffed her shirt. "Is there a new shirt in one of these boxes?"

"Stop it. Put the bag away."

"Hey, there's a little box at the bottom."

I pulled the truck off the road and stopped. "Give me the bag."

She wrapped her arms around it. "You said these are for me."

"They're Christmas presents. The operative word being Christmas. Hand me the bag. I'm putting it in the back seat."

She handed me the bag and pretended to pout. "You're getting a lump of coal."

I pulled back on the road and glanced at her. "You really are a little kid when it comes to Christmas."

Jill let out a breath. "It was the one time I was special. I got presents and was treated as Jill and not the half of the twins who didn't die. So, yes, Christmas is very special." She unbuckled her seatbelt and slid to the center of the bench seat and buckled in there. "And I'm very pleased to have someone special to share it with this year."

"What have you done for Christmas the past few years?"

"I opened my presents from Mom and Dad, then went to a Chinese restaurant for supper."

"That seems sad."

She pulled my arm over her shoulder. "What did you do?"

"About the same thing. I opened my present from Mom, then called her and left a message because she was celebrating with her friends or our extended family."

"Was it hard not to crack open a bottle and start drinking?"

"The simple answer is yes."

"And the not so simple answer?"

"It was tempting to drive to a bar and hang out with the other people who had nowhere to go on Christmas. Or, walk to Sheila's house and have a beer or a cup of coffee."

"Either of those could've spiraled out of control."

"Yes. That's why I'd watch an old movie until I fell asleep on the couch."

"Doug…"

"What?"

"I don't care if the bedsprings squeak or not."

"You do know that your parents and my mother will all be there to hear them tonight."

"Oh, no. Ronnie will be right across the hall."

"Yes, she will. And we know her hearing is excellent because she pointed out that the Mustang Island walls are paper thin."

"We may have to come up with an excuse to rent a motel room."

"You smell like a manure pile and need a shower. Is that enough excuse?"

"We have to go to the ranch. Your mother is there and Mom's got supper cooking."

"You're sure…"

"I might be persuaded if I could open that little box in the bottom of the shopping bag."

We were both laughing when we pulled onto the interstate in Rapid City.

* * *

Molly met us on the steps and took one whiff of Jill and clenched her eyes shut. "What kind of manure were you rolling in?"

"It's a long story, Mom."

"Get yourself into the shower and throw your clothes into the hallway. I'll put them right into the washer." She looked at me. "And Doug, say hi to your mom, then get Jill something to wear that doesn't stink to high heaven."

Jill waved as she scooted past through the kitchen and into the bathroom.

Al spun to watch her and then looked at me. "What happened to her?"

I pecked Mom's cheek and sat down at the table, taking in the wonderful cooking smells coming from the stove. "Jill was in Wind Cave searching for a missing woman today and she crawled through some bat…droppings. She's a little gamy right now and needs a shower really badly." Mom was smiling and looked very content. "How was your flight?"

"Smooth as glass. I closed my eyes when we took off and didn't open them again until the wheels touched down. Molly and Al were waiting for me by the luggage carousel. They scooped me up, drove me here, and Al carried my suitcase into the spare bedroom."

I heard the shower start, then the bathroom door opened and closed. Molly hustled down the hallway with a plastic garbage bag.

"I think that's my cue to find Jill some fresh clothes. Excuse me for a minute." I pulled fresh clothes out of Jill's suitcase and made a neat pile on the bed. Steam billowed from the bathroom as I set the fresh clothes on the sink. "Are you doing okay?"

Jill pulled back a corner of the shower curtain and peeked out. Her hair was lathered with shampoo. "I'm fine, but the longer I stand here the more I smell the stink. I'll rinse out the shampoo and be out in a minute."

There was a steaming cup of cocoa next to the open bag of marshmallows on the table by my chair. Al had dark liquid in a lowball glass. Mom and Molly were drinking cocoa. Jill came out of the shower running her fingers through her short hair. She bent down, hugged my mother, and kissed her cheek. "Welcome to the ranch, Ronnie."

Mom stood up and hugged Jill. "It was very kind of your mom and dad to include me in their Christmas celebration. It'll be fun."

There was a knock on the door and Chet, Al and Molly's neighbor, stepped in without waiting for an invitation. He took off his Stetson and hung it and his sheepskin coat behind the door. "Hey, folks," he said as he pulled off his boots exposing one sock with a big hole in the toe.

Molly got up and took down a mug and a lowball glass. "I assume you'd prefer bourbon to cocoa, Chet."

Chet smiled and pecked Molly on the cheek. "You know me well." He handed her a bag of plastic containers she'd previously sent home filled with leftovers.

I stood and shook his hand and Jill hugged him. "Chet, this is Ronnie, Doug's mother. Ronnie, this is Chet, our neighbor and my adopted uncle."

Ronnie stood and Chet gently shook her hand. "Pleased to meet you, ma'am." He looked at Ronnie for a second, then at me. "I can see where Doug got his good looks."

Mom smiled. "You're very generous with your praise."

Molly handed him a glass half-full of bourbon. "Your son is one hell of a good shot," Chet said as he sat down.

Mom looked at me. "You've been shooting with Chet?"

Chet nodded. "I've never seen anyone make a smiley face on a target before. He's damned...darned good."

Mom cocked her head. "A smiley face on a target?"

Chet took a swig of booze. "Yes ma'am. He fired off six shots as fast as he could pull the trigger and that old target got two eyes, a nose, and a smile."

I didn't react, but Jill nodded. "He's that good, Ronnie."

"I suppose that's quite a compliment."

"Yep, it is," Chet added. "Too bad he can't ride."

"Well, Chet, there aren't many horses in St. Paul where Doug grew up."

"I heard that, ma'am."

Mom reached out and put her hand on Chet's. I saw in his eyes that he was unprepared for her touch. "Chet, please call me Ronnie."

Chet looked at her hand, then looked up. "I'd be proud to call you Ronnie, if that's what you'd prefer."

"I much prefer Ronnie to ma'am. Somehow ma'am seems like a title for my mother."

Chet's head nodded. "I meant no..."

"I know you were being polite, and I appreciate that. But we're among friends here, and Ronnie is what my friends call me."

"Yes, ma'am…Ronnie. It might take me a bit to get used to that. Forgive me if slip up."

Mom patted his hand. "There's no forgiveness required for being gentlemanly, Chet."

Molly pulled a Dutch oven out of the stove and lifted the lid. The browning meat and onions flooded the room. "I hope everyone likes Swiss steak and mashed potatoes."

Chet smiled. "Molly, I like anything you make." He looked at Mom. "Molly's the best cook in the county."

Jill got up and took a potato masher out of a drawer. "I've got the potatoes. What else do you need, Mom?"

"All I've got to do is drain the asparagus. Doug, would you set the table?"

Mom stood. "What can I do to help, Molly?"

Molly waved off her assistance. "You sit there and make sure Al and Chet don't start telling bawdy stories about the old days."

Mom sat down and grinned. "I might enjoy a bawdy story."

Chet laughed. "Ronnie, the stories Molly's talking about aren't fit for polite company."

We chatted through supper and the Mom of old returned, laughing at stories from Molly, Chet and Al, and telling a few stories of her own. Jill glanced at me a couple times to see if I was holding up okay because a few of Mom's stories were about my teen past and revealed a bit more than I'd ever shared with Jill.

At Thanksgiving, Chet had taken me aside and proclaimed his affection for Jill and his disappointment that she's married me, an outsider, when he'd planned to "woo" her at some future point when he felt it wouldn't be seen as cradle-robbing by the other neighbors. Chet was polite to Jill, but like an uncle, not a suitor. Molly broke out sherry after supper. Chet and Al had already downed at least three rounds of bourbon. We toasted Ronnie's visit and Christmas. Chet's cheeks were rosy, and his attention became focused on Mom.

When Molly emptied the last of the sherry into Al and Mom's glasses, Chet looked at his watch. "I should let you folks go to bed."

Molly put three containers of leftovers in a paper bag while Chet put on his boots, hat, and coat. "I thank you kindly for the hospitality and the leftovers."

We all walked to the door. Al and I shook Chet's hand. Molly and Jill hugged him, and there was an awkward second where Chet was trying to decide if he should shake Mom's hand, tip his hat, or just escape.

Mom stepped up and hugged him, then pecked his cheek, which caused him to turn red. "Goodnight, Chet. I can see why you're so special to the Rickowskis."

Chet nodded, obviously tongue-tied, and slipped out he door.

Ronnie helped Molly wash and dry the sherry glasses, then said it was bedtime. I hugged Jill as Mom closed the bedroom door. "I think Chet took a shine to Mom."

Jill grinned. "I think the pressure is off you. Chet seemed to accept that you weren't going to step aside so he could woo me."

I heard bedsprings squeak as Mom sat on the guest bed and I laughed. "We'll know every time she rolls over all night long."

I took Jill's hand and turned toward the bedroom.

Molly's voice stopped me. "Doug, did you notice the cardboard and plastic piled next to the burning barrel?"

"No. I didn't."

Molly smiled. "It's from the new mattress and box spring on Jill's bed. I checked—it doesn't squeak."

Jill's elbow poked me gently in the ribs. "Don't say a word," she whispered.

I looked at Al who was smiling. He raised his eyes suggestively and turned on the news.

Jill's childhood bedroom had become "our" bedroom at the ranch. It was always chilly, and with the outside temperature dipping well below zero, it was downright frosty. Jill took a nightgown and left for the bathroom, being uncomfortable being seen naked. I changed into a pair of flannel pants and a long-sleeved t-shirt, then slipped into the cold sheets. Jill turned off the lights when she came into the room and closed the door behind her. I felt the bed shift, but not squeak, as she sat on the edge. She pulled up the sheet and quilt, then pressed herself against my back.

"I haven't warmed up since I got out of the cave. Generate some body heat."

She put her arm over me and slipped her hand under my shirt, running her fingers through my chest hair. I rolled over and realized she was naked beside me.

"You're going to freeze without your flannel nightgown," I said, running my hand over the goosebumps on her arm.

"You told Rachel we were like two logs that generate more heat together than either of us apart."

"That was a metaphor for our love. I wasn't talking about actual heat. And when did you hear that?"

"Rachel told me that while she was staying with Mandy and Matt. That thought helped her understand what we had, and what was lacking in her relationship with her ex-boyfriend. Whether you knew it or not, those were powerful words."

Jill tugged at the hem of my t-shirt, pulling it up. "Let's test the bedsprings."

I pulled the shirt over my head and tossed it on the floor. "Are you trying to seduce me?"

"I'd say it's not going to take a lot of seduction. Part of you seems to be responding without a lot of provocation."

Chapter Eight

December 23rd

Our mothers were drinking coffee and eating cinnamon rolls. There was a platter of warm rolls in the middle of the table and the icing was running off them and collecting on the platter. Jill was in the shower and I got a mug of coffee.

Molly and Ronnie had been talking and they looked between each other before Molly said, "I hope you got some sleep last night."

I used a fork to pull a roll off the platter. "Please don't embarrass Jill." I put the roll on a plate, then pulled free an outer layer that was warm to my touch.

Mom reached over and put her hand on mine. "Douglas, I have no intention of embarrassing Jill. What I'm…we're telling you is that we're pleased that you two have found each other and…"

Molly interrupted. "Doug, you two spent half a lifetime too tied up in your careers to make room for love. Show each other your love every chance you get in any way you can."

Jill walked in fluffing her damp hair and froze. "Are we having the squeaking spring talk again?" She paused. "And Ronnie, you're in on it too?"

Mom got up and hugged Jill. "Make the springs squeak while you can, dear."

"I'm not having this discussion with my mother and mother-in-law. What's for breakfast?"

Jill got a mug out of the cupboard and poured herself coffee.

I could tell Mom had something more to say. "Let it go, Mom."

She put up her hand, tried to say something but started laughing. She put on a sober face and looked at Jill. "I might've brought a jar of passionfruit jam."

Molly and Mom laughed while Jill stabbed a cinnamon roll. "I feel like I'm back in junior high school."

My cellphone rang and I walked to the living room to answer it without checking the caller ID.

"Fletcher."

I recognized Jess Pond's voice. "Hi, Doug. We were busy last night, and I think we have a lead. I talked to the banker in Mitchell, and they're leaving the victim's debit card active for another day. The card was used at another ATM last night. The guy is cagey, and had his face obscured, but he took his glove off to take the cash. He's got an unusual tattoo on his wrist. I've got an agent ready to hit the local tattoo parlors to see if any of the artists recognize the design and can tie it to a customer."

"That's a start. Jill and I spoke with a Custer County deputy yesterday. He suggested that the woman might be a prostitute the victim picked up, and the guy with the charge card might be her partner."

"That would be an interesting twist. I'm talking and thinking at the same time, so bear with me. It seems a little unlikely that he'd pick up a hooker who'd stay around with him. Our experience has been that they want to make their money and move on to another customer."

"Yeah, Butch, the deputy we spoke to, talked about the women who show up during Sturgis bike week and move from one campsite to the next. I think he called them 'tent bunnies' because they hop around."

"Do you remember that movie, 'Pretty Woman?' People watched that and now they think all prostitutes look like Julia Roberts and they hang around with their customers for the weekend. The reality is that many of them are hard drug users, are hooking to support their habit and an abusive boyfriend or pimp, and often have some STI they've contracted from their drug use or an infected customer."

"Gee, Jess, you make it sound so romantic."

"That's the bottom line; there is no romance involved." Jess paused. "So, we're looking for a tattoo artist and checking the bars around the

SDSM&T campus. What's the National Park Service doing today?"

"Chris Ostberg has three teams of rangers searching the more remote parts of the cave. They won't get to the farthest reaches, but they'll cover most of the likely areas a woman on the run might've gone, and they'll be looking for a woman's footprints. Jill and I are going to show the victim's picture to the bars and stores in Keystone to see if anyone recognizes him, hoping they might have surveillance video of the girl."

"Be sure to check the gas stations and pharmacies, too."

"Why?" I asked.

"He probably needed gas after driving here from Mitchell, and gas stations always have surveillance cameras inside and out. Pharmacies have cameras, and if this couple were practicing safe sex, they bought condoms."

"Okay. We'll call if we stumble across anything more."

"Unless we hit a really hot lead, my people are off tomorrow and Christmas Day. I suggest you guys plan to hunker down tomorrow night and all Christmas Day. Denver is already cancelling Christmas Eve flights ahead of the blizzard and it'll be here by tomorrow night. I'm not planning to stick my nose out the door until the roads are plowed."

"Merry Christmas, Jess."

"We'll talk again before then, but Merry Christmas to you and Jill, too."

I shut down the call and topped off my mug with warm coffee.

Al had joined the table while I was on the phone. "Sounds like your dead guy might've been with a lady of the evening."

"That's a quaint description," I said as I sat down to finish my roll.

"That's what we used to call them."

Molly scowled. "How would you know about that, Al?"

"I get around. Besides, I just overheard Doug talking about shady women."

"Jill and I have our marching orders for today. The FBI says they're going to be off Christmas Eve and Day, and that the weather will probably shut down everything tomorrow night."

Al welcomed the change of topic. "The forecasters are saying this is going to be a big one. We'll probably get hit pretty hard here." He turned to Mother. "Ronnie, it looks like you get to experience a real South Dakota blizzard."

Mom looked less than enthused. "Oh, boy."

I started the truck and went back in the house while it warmed up. Molly and Mom were clearing the breakfast dishes while I rubbed my hands, trying to warm them after scraping the windshield.

"Do you want to take some sandwiches?" Molly asked.

"Thanks, but we'll grab lunch at a restaurant."

Molly shook her head. "You've been away from the north country too long. You need to have a blizzard kit in that truck you're driving. I'll put together a bag with matches, a couple candles, sandwiches, candy bars, and a jug of water. Fill up your gas tank if it gets below three-quarters full. If you drive into a ditch somewhere, you'll be prepared until a tow truck can get to you."

"We've got cellphones. We'll be okay."

"No, Doug," Molly said. "You don't understand. When the weather gets bad, they pull the plows, tow trucks and highway patrol off and close the roads. If you're in a ditch somewhere, you could be there for two or more days."

I nodded rather than contesting the point. Jill came out with two quilts I'd seen on the closet shelf. "We'll put these in the backseat, too."

Heeding Molly's advice, I topped off the pickup's gas tanks in Rapid City while Jill cleaned the windows and headlights with a half-frozen scrubber/scraper. I paid with my federal credit card and bought four bottles of water to keep in the truck, knowing they'd be frozen overnight. I showed the driver's license photo of our victim to the three people working at the truck stop, but none of them recognized him. One suggested I come back earlier in the morning and in the evening to catch the clerks who worked those shifts because they were open 24/7 and there were nearly two dozen employees who might've seen our victim. Another clerk suggested I look for Santa Claus, because he said he'd be more likely to remember someone in a red suit than an average-looking guy among the several hundred average guys he saw a day.

We were in Keystone, near the entrance to Mount Rushmore, mid-morning as the stores were opening. Jill started at the south end of town and I drove to the center, parked, and worked north on the left side of the highway. A few of the touristy places were closed for the winter, but I was able to show the picture to five store clerks and a few customers before noon. My phone rang at almost exactly noon.

"Hey, I'm at the pickup and my cinnamon roll is long gone. Let's meet at the pizza and chicken place in the mall on the east side of the highway. Their sign says they have a salad bar and I'd really like to eat something leafy and green."

The restaurant was cozy and homey with a bar top made from a thick slab of pine. The finish made it look like it was wet. There were only five other customers.

We sat at a table in the back, facing the door. "I wonder if they make enough to cover the overhead."

Jill looked around. "This looks like the kind of place that'll attract an after-school crowd for pizza and soda pop."

Our waitress was barely out of high school, with a friendly smile and twinkling eyes. "Can I get you something to drink?"

"Diet Coke for both of us."

Jill looked around. "Your sign says you have a salad bar."

"I'm sorry, we only set that up in the evenings during the winter." She handed us menus. "The cook can whip up a great chef salad."

Jill smiled and handed the menu back. "I'd like that with ranch dressing."

The waitress looked at me. "Are you ready, sir?"

"Give me a minute to look over the menu."

Jill shook her head. "You know, a chef salad wouldn't kill you."

I folded the menu and set it on the table as our perky waitress brought our drinks. "Have you made up your mind, sir?"

"He's having a chef salad."

"What dressing would you like?"

I let out a sigh. "Surprise me."

Our waitress looked stricken. "Sir?"

"Doug, quit being a jerk," Jill hissed.

Our waitress read the interchange and regained her composure. "Maybe you'd like a side salad with something else, sir?"

Jill closed her eyes. "Go ahead. Get something greasy and salty."

The waitress looked hopeful that I'd let her off the hook. "We make the best pizza in Keystone."

I refrained from asking how many places served pizza but decided to be civil. "Pepperoni and green pepper pizza with a side salad. Do you have a house dressing?"

"We have a really good balsamic vinaigrette."

"I'll go with that."

Our perky waitress nearly ran away, like she'd been released from purgatory. "That was pathetic." Jill paused and cocked her elbow. "I dare you to say, 'yes dear.'"

"I wasn't trying to be contrary. I just didn't want a chef salad." I read her look of disgust. "Listen to yourself. You told me you weren't planning to change me. That we were set in our ways and we needed to adapt, not try to rebuild."

Jill thought for a second, then nodded. "Yes, but I want you to be with me for a long time. I think we could maximize that time together if your diet had a few more fruits and vegetables."

I smiled. "I asked for green peppers on my pizza."

"Yes, you're having a side salad. I get it. You're trying."

"Tell me you're not going to eat a slice of pizza."

Jill smiled in surrender. "Only to save you from having to eat it all yourself."

"Did you get any hits on the picture?"

"Nobody recognized the guy. I'll go to a couple of the hotels, but since he was camping, I don't really expect success with that."

"Yeah, that might be an exercise in futility. Come along with me while I hit the bars and stores on this side of the street. If we strike out there, we'll head back to Custer."

Our salads arrived. Jill's salad was in a serving bowl and could've easily fed both of us. She surveyed it, trying to decide where she could stick a fork in it without having salad spilling on the table. She gave up, stuck her fork in, and a handful of lettuce fell on the table. I poured dressing on my salad and was about to dig in when my phone buzzed.

"Fletcher," I said, standing up and walking toward the bathrooms in the back.

"Doug, this is Butch Henson, in Custer."

"Yeah, Butch, what can I do for you?"

"Actually, it's what I might be able to do for you. I've been showing your picture around town and not getting anywhere. I was talking to the county attorney and he suggested that I pull up pictures of young women we've arrested in the past year and take them to Flora. Maybe she'll recognize one of them as the woman with your dead guy."

"That's a great idea. We're just eating lunch in Keystone. Can we meet you in an hour or so?"

"You'd better make it two hours. I've got to pick up a prisoner in Rapid City, but I should be back by three o'clock."

"Great, Butch, I'll see you at three."

It was hard to see that Jill had made a dent in her salad while I was gone. "Who called?"

"Butch is meeting us at three in Custer." I explained Butch's plan.

My pizza was smaller than Jill's salad. Our waitress looked hopeful that Jill wasn't going to throw a fit. Sensing her anxiety, Jill slipped her fork under an edge piece and pulled it onto a spare plate. That move broke the tension.

"I'll grab refills for your soda pop. Can I get you anything else?"

Jill took a bite of pizza and burned her lips. She waved off the question.

"That was smooth," I said.

"That poor girl looked like her knees were knocking."

I took a bite of salad, then pushed the bowl aside and pulled the pizza close. Jill shook her head but was smiling.

Our waitress came back with our refreshed drinks. Then she surprised me by pulling out a chair and sitting down. "I saw your badges. Are you guys rangers?"

"We're law enforcement rangers with the National Park Service. Can we help you?"

"I didn't know the National Park Service had their own cops. I was just curious." She looked around the room to see if the other customers needed her. Everything must've been under control because she stayed seated. "We get rangers in here, but they're usually in uniforms, not jeans and boots."

"We can wear civilian clothes when we're investigating."

"You showed me a guy's picture. What are you investigating?"

"A visitor died at Wind Cave last week. We're trying to determine what happened to him."

"I heard he was attacked by a mountain lion."

"That's what it looks like, but someone stole his pickup and wallet. His cards are getting used in Rapid City."

"Yeah, we get some bogus cards here sometimes. VISA is really good and pays if we get a bounce back on a charge."

Jill wiped her mouth. "Have you had a charge bounce recently?"

"There was a couple in here last week who paid for a pizza with a bogus card. I was suspicious because the logo on the card didn't look right, but the card worked when I ran it."

I pulled out my phone and showed her the picture of the dead guy again. "He wasn't the guy?"

"Nah. Not even close. Your guy looks like a geek. The girl had the card and the guy looked more like a biker."

Jill was very interested. "Do you have a record of the name on the card that bounced?"

"I think it's behind the counter. Let me check."

"Here it is. Brigette Daly."

"Describe her?"

143

She looked like a college student. Young, kinda blonde, kinda cute."

"How tall?"

"She was sitting down, so I couldn't tell."

"Do you remember what she was wearing?" Jill asked.

"Jeans, like everyone here."

"How about her top? Sweatshirt? Tank top? Jacket?"

"It was just a week ago, so it wasn't a tank top or anything skimpy. I don't remember exactly what she had on. But the guy was wearing a leather vest over a black tee."

"Hair color? Eyes? Moustache? Scars? Tattoos?"

"He had long hair, a dark beard and moustache, all kinda shaggy. Tats all over his arms. There was something off about them, like the girl had done something wrong and he was mad at her."

I got up. "You guys keep talking. I'll be right back." I walked near the bathroom and punched in Jess Pond's cell number.

"What's up, Doug?"

"Can you send me a text with the tattoo picture from the ATM?"

"Sure. Hang on,"

Less than ten seconds later my phone dinged. I opened the text showing a man's hand with a strange assortment of disconnected pieces, some that appeared to be paisley.

"Got it."

"What's up?"

"I'm in Keystone and a waitress remembers a couple who were in here last week. The woman used a bogus credit card with Brigette Daly's name. I've got a vague description of the girl, but she remembers the guy having long dark hair, a beard and moustache, and tattoos on his arms. I want to show her this."

"Let me know if you get anything from her."

I closed the call and went back to the table. Jill was sitting alone eating pizza.

"Where's our waitress?"

"She's trying to get the video overlooking the cash register."

"Good call." I took a piece of pizza and looked at Jill's half eaten salad. "You gave up on the salad?"

"My jaw got tired of chewing." She held up a half-eaten wedge of pizza. "And the pizza tastes good. Who did you call?"

I opened the text from Jess and showed Jill the image of the ATM bandit's hand.

"It's kind of hard to tell what it's supposed to be. I suppose it's something abstract and we aren't seeing enough of it to make sense of the pieces."

The waitress came back with a thumb drive. "Here's a copy of the security video. Do you have a computer to open it?"

"Not here. Can you print a copy of the picture?" Jill asked.

"We don't have a printer. I guess you'll have to take it somewhere."

145

I turned my phone so the waitress could see the picture from the ATM. "Does this look familiar?"

She studied the image. "It sorta does, but I can't remember how. These pieces were part of a bigger tattoo that went up the guy's arm." She turned the image and her eyes lit up. "See these blobs that kinda look like tear drops? They're claws from a scorpion. Most of the scorpion went up the guy's arm but the claws ended on his wrist."

"I've got to make another call. Can you show my partner the video?"

I dialed Jess. "Our waitress says we're looking at the claws from a scorpion. The scorpion's body was on the guy's forearm."

"Got it. I'll have Gloria start making calls immediately."

"We've also got security camera video but it's on a thumb drive and we don't have any way to view it and the restaurant doesn't have a printer. We're meeting a Custer County deputy in an hour. I'm sure he'll be able to open the file and send you a copy."

"Get it to me ASAP. My people will be out of here at five and won't be back for three days, maybe longer depending on the snowstorm."

"I promise you'll have it as soon as I get it, Jess."

Jill came back holding her phone. "I took a video of the playback. It's tiny and grainy, but at least I've got images of the two people."

"Send it to Jess and me. I'll forward it on to Butch too."

By the time I got back to the table Jill's salad and my pizza were boxed up and Jill was signing a charge slip. "I'm leaving her a twenty-dollar tip."

"That'll probably double her tip income for the day," I said.

Jill got up and picked up the Styrofoam take-out containers. "I certainly hope it makes her Christmas just a little merrier."

* * *

Jill was shopping the sales in the back with Flora's coaching while I paced by the front door. I watched Butch park and met him at the door.

He held out several pages of printouts, each with pictures of six young blonde women. Some looked like they'd just walked out of homeroom. Others looked hard, tired, and angry. "Maybe one of these women is our shopper. Where's Flora?"

"She's guiding my partner through the sale racks in the back."

Butch smiled. "Your partner, as in Jill, your wife?"

I nodded and showed Butch the picture of the scorpion's claw from the ATM. "I may have another piece of the puzzle. That picture was taken at an ATM in Rapid City. The card was skimmed from a card reader. A Keystone waitress recognized it as part of a scorpion tattoo on a customer's arm. He was there about a week ago with a young woman who charged their lunch with the same card used here, at Flora's. She described the guy as looking like a biker with long dark hair and a full beard."

Butch looked impressed. "You guys are covering a lot of ground."

"The FBI got the ATM picture for us. As you know, the rest of our job is pounding the pavement trying to find that one piece of the puzzle that makes the others fit into place."

I led Butch to the back of Flora's. Jill was trying on a pair of cowboy boots while Flora held the box. "Are you going to buy these for Christmas too? They're my size."

Flora smiled and winked at me. I assumed that meant she hadn't spilled what I'd purchased in my earlier trip. "The other boxes might be boots. You'd better put those back until after Christmas."

Jill stood up and took a few steps. "The other boxes are too flat to be boots."

"Butch has some pictures for Flora."

Flora flipped through the pages of photos quickly, shaking her head. "She's not any of these women."

Butch looked at me. "It would've been almost too easy if this had been the answer."

Jill flipped through the photos. "Just because she hasn't been arrested here doesn't mean she's never been arrested."

Butch took the pictures back. "True, but without a fingerprint or DNA, I don't know how else we're going to identify her."

"Maybe the FBI will be able to find the artist who did the scorpion tattoo," I said.

Jill took off the boots and handed them to Flora. "Well, big spender, are you buying the boots for me or am I paying for them myself?"

"Like I said, it's too close to Christmas to be buying stuff."

Flora took Jill's charge card and walked to the cash register in the front. Jill whispered, "Cheapskate," as she passed.

Butch watched the exchange and smiled. "There's no way you were going to win that one, Fletcher."

I walked past him and snatched Jill's charge card out of Flora's hand before she could put it in the reader. I handed it back to Jill and pulled out my VISA card. "Please gift wrap those and make sure there aren't any loose edges that might 'accidentally' rip open before Christmas."

Butch slapped me on the shoulder. "Nice recovery. Not much of a surprise for Christmas, but my wife prefers picking out her own gifts rather than hoping for the best with me."

Flora handed me the receipt for a signature. "Actually Butch, you had incredibly good taste this year. And I need your VISA card for the charge."

Butch dug out his wallet. "Are the packages here or did she take them home already?"

Flora cocked her head. "You didn't notice them under the tree?"

"Did she pick out anything for me, or do I need to buy something for myself?"

"You're covered, as are the kids and your grandson."

"I hope I've got enough left on my credit card to cover it all."

Flora put the card in the reader. "You're good, but you might want to pay down your bill before Valentine's Day."

We watched Flora wrap Jill's boots. Butch put his credit card away, handed me a business card, and shook my hand. "If you need anything else, call. I'm on night shift both Christmas Eve and Day. It'll be quiet except for when the bars close, so I wouldn't mind a call."

I dug the thumb drive from my pocket and handed it to Butch. "Here's video of the biker and girl from the pizza place. I've got no way to view it."

Butch slipped it in his pocket. "I'll email a copy to you when I get to a computer."

I carried the bag with the boots to the pickup and put them in the back seat. "I guess my Christmas shopping is done."

Jill gave me a sly smile that made me uneasy. "You don't believe that do you?"

"Why wouldn't I think I was done?"

"What have you got for your mother?"

"We don't usually exchange gifts."

"So, she'll be really surprised when you pull out a nice present."

"What do you have in mind?"

"It's already in the bag with the boots."

"What did I buy her?"

"*We* bought her a Black Hills gold necklace and a pair of turquoise earrings."

I leaned over and kissed Jill. "Thank you. What did we get for your parents?"

"My mother is getting a bracelet with our birthstones."

"Our birthstones?"

"Diamonds and sapphires. She asked for something that would remind her of us."

"How much…"

I got a look that would melt steel. "Suck it up. It'll all be worth it when you see the look on her face when she opens it."

"That's a lot more than you spent on my mom."

Jill grinned. "I didn't say the necklace and earrings were the only things we got your mother."

"How about your dad?"

Jill pointed down the street. "Jack Daniels."

We walked into the liquor store and the clerk nodded to us, seemingly unconcerned about the unknown man and woman who'd walked past him with the bulge of guns on our belts. I found the section of whiskey and bourbon and surveyed the shelf. I took down a 1.75-liter bottle of Gentleman Jack.

"Is that really good?" Jill asked.

"I couldn't afford it when I was drinking, so I expect it is."

Jill took down a second bottle.

"We're each getting him one?" I asked.

Jill shook her head. "This one's for Uncle Chet."

The gray-haired clerk looked up from the newspaper. "Y'all done?"

We set the two bottles on the counter. "That's all that's left on our Christmas list."

The clerk looked at us and paused. "You saw the price on these?"

I nodded and handed him my Visa card. He smiled. "I wish I was on your shopping list."

"Can you wrap those?" I asked.

The corner of his mouth twitched. "I tell people I don't, but most folks don't spend a day's wages on a couple bottles of really good booze." He reached under the counter and pulled out a pair of red gift bags. After he handed back my card, he put the bottles in the bags and then put them in a larger shopping bag.

"Merry Christmas," I said as he handed us the bags.

"I probably don't need to tell you this, but don't drink all that in one day."

Jill smiled. "I suspect my father will keep this on a shelf for years just so he can show his rancher friends what a nice gift his daughter and son-in-law gave him."

The store owner smiled.

As we walked back to the pickup I asked, "Will Chet drink his all in one sitting?"

"I doubt it. He'll probably crack it open at Mom and Daddy's house to be sociable, then sip the rest of it at home in the evenings."

"Chet comes over for Christmas?"

Jill pulled me close. "Uncle Chet's been at our house for Christmas every year for as long as I can remember. Mom has pictures of me sitting on Uncle Chet's lap opening a doll when I was four or five and that wasn't his first Christmas with us."

"Junior was on his other knee?"

I felt Jill tense. "Junior was always on Daddy's knee and I was on Uncle Chet's."

"I feel like I just scraped off a scab."

"It'd be best if Junior didn't come up over the holidays."

My phone buzzed and I handed the bag to Jill. "Fletcher."

"We scored on the scorpion tattoo. An artist in Sturgis has seen them, although he's never done one himself. It's the logo for the Scorpions. They're a biker gang out of Denver. We've been digging through the internet for an hour after talking to the Denver FBI office. They're as bad as they come."

"Hang on for a second, Jess. Jill and I are walking to the pickup. I'd like to put you on speaker so Jill can hear you." I unlocked the pickup and set the cellphone on the dashboard. "Okay Jess, repeat what you just said."

"The Scorpions are a biker gang based in Denver although they have their fingers in bad stuff all over the region. They started out dealing drugs, then moved into distribution after a couple of their guys got sent up. They're supposed to be in everything from human trafficking to contract murder, but they've had good lawyers. A few witnesses have disappeared before trials and a few others have recanted before testifying."

"Would you expect one of them to be hanging around this area?"

"There are all kinds of rumors about what might be going on locally. One that we hear most often is that Rapid City is a regional distribution hub for meth coming out of Mexico. So, I guess it wouldn't be surprising that one or more of the Scorpions would be hanging around here. Then there's the traffic on the interstate that attracts a certain number of men looking for female companionship while they're away from home."

"Would they be brazen enough to use a stolen card at an ATM?"

"He's been cagey, and we haven't seen his face. I suppose he didn't think someone might identify the scorpion tattoo from the little bit visible on the back of his hand."

"I guess it's working because even though we think he's part of the gang, we haven't seen his face." I paused. "But I've got a waitress who saw him. Can you get some booking pictures from Denver?"

"I can do better than that. We have booking pictures of a few of the guys who've been arrested, but the Denver office has had them under surveillance, and I have candid photos of virtually all the gang members."

"Can you text or email them to me?"

"They'll be on your phone within the hour."

Jill looked at me after I shut down the call. "Are we going back to Keystone?" She checked her watch. "It'll be six o'clock before we get there."

I made a U-turn in the street and accelerated. "Cops don't get to punch time clocks when an investigation is hot."

Jill pulled out her cellphone. "Mom, we're going to be really late. Eat supper without us."

I caught parts of Molly's side of the conversation and heard something about red velvet cake. Jill put her phone in her pocket. "Mom wasn't happy that we're abandoning them. She made pork roast with apples and roasted potatoes. She said she'll try to keep a couple pieces of red velvet cake for us, but Daddy and Uncle Chet have been known to eat nearly a whole cake in one sitting."

"Call the pizza restaurant and see if our waitress is still there. If she's gone for the day there's not much point in rushing to Keystone."

Our waitress was on her way out the door. She wasn't willing to stay around to look at biker pictures, and she wasn't willing to give Jill her home address, email, or phone number.

I slowed and handed Jill my phone. "Call Butch, get his email address, and forward Jess' file with the photos to him. Ask him to show the pictures to the hotels, bars, and restaurants while he's bored over Christmas."

Jill punched a number into her phone, and I expected her to have a conversation with Butch. I was surprised when she said, "Hi, Mom. Change of plans. We're on our way." She listened and nodded. "Yes, it was the threat of the red velvet cake that changed Doug's mind."

She gave me a sly look as she dialed Butch's cellphone. They had a short conversation and Jill emailed the biker pictures to him.

We were just outside Rapid City when my cellphone buzzed. I didn't look at the caller ID, assuming it was Molly checking on our arrival time.

"Hey, Doug," Chris Ostberg said. "Is Jill with you?"

"Hang on. I'll put you on speaker." I touched the speaker icon and handed the phone to Jill. "We're in the pickup on our way back to Spearfish. We can talk as long as we have cell service."

"I had three teams in the caves, and we went as far in as we can get in a one-day hike. We didn't find the missing woman or any sign of her. The further we got in, the fewer footprints we found and, to be frank, there weren't any woman's footprints that looked like they'd been made by anything but a hiking boot, and there were very few of those. I can say with virtually one hundred percent certainty that your missing woman is not in the cave unless she went in some opening that hasn't been discovered in the last hundred fifty years."

"I guess we can close the book on that option."

"I think so, too. I assume you guys are hunkering down at the ranch ahead of the blizzard."

"That's our plan. I'll keep you updated if we develop any new leads."

"Merry Christmas, guys. I'm sending my people home and barricading the gate until after the storm. Be safe and stay warm."

Chapter Nine

Chet's pickup was in Rickowski's driveway with a horse trailer hooked behind it. I could smell the pork roast from the sidewalk outside the house. The family was still sitting around the table, but the pork roast was seriously damaged and there weren't many browned potatoes left. We hung out coats behind the door and Jill set our shopping bags under the side table next to the kitchen counter.

Molly looked over her shoulder at the bag. "Looks like you have been shopping more than investigating."

I pulled up a chair. "We've managed to get in some of each."

Chet handed me the platter of meat and Jill scooped a potato onto her plate before handing me the bowl with the last potato.

Ronnie slid a gravy boat to me. "I didn't expect to see you two before bedtime."

"Things changed. The waitress we wanted to interview was gone for the day."

"I hope she has the good sense to stay home until after the storm."

I looked at Jill, having forgotten about the impending blizzard. "I suppose we're not going to catch many people around their businesses for a few days."

Jill shrugged. "They'll be there after the blizzard."

I was unaccustomed to doing anything but sprint after a case when I had leads, so her comments caught me by surprise. I was going to say something, then realized that we were on the cusp of Christmas and a storm that was probably going to shut down everything. There was nothing I could do to change the situation.

Jill sensed my anxiety, and I felt her stocking rubbing the top of my foot. I relaxed and realized Al had asked me a question.

"Sorry Al, I checked out for a second. What did you ask?"

"What do your Texas friends do for Christmas? I don't imagine there are a lot of pine trees down there. Do they decorate palm trees and cactus?"

"I don't know. We haven't been there over the holidays. Maybe we'll stay down there next Christmas."

Chet surprised me when he spoke up. "Doug, I haven't had any family but the Rickowski's for my whole adult life. Let me give you a piece of advice; spend time with your family while you've got the chance. If not for Al, Molly, and Jill, my holidays would've been pretty bleak for the last fifty years."

I looked at my mother who was staring into her coffee cup. She glanced up and I realized I'd abandoned her at Christmas, and every holiday, for several years. I'd called, but it had never occurred to me that I should've flown to St. Paul.

Molly gathered the empty plates. On her way back to the table, she leaned over my shoulder and whispered in my ear. "I hope you feel like this is home. You, Jill, and Ronnie are always…always welcome here."

I turned my head and kissed her cheek. "Thank you. And thanks for including Mom."

Jill got small plates out of the cupboard and Ronnie uncovered a beautifully frosted cake. She cut a piece and slid the red-colored cake with white cream cheese frosting onto a plate and passed it to my mother. "For our guest of honor."

Chet faked indignance. "I thought I was the guest of honor!"

"Chet, you're family, not a guest. If you think you're anyone but Al's long-lost brother, you're mistaken." She passed cake to Chet.

"Well, if I'm family, I expect a present this year."

Al slapped his knee. "Chet, you get the same present from us every year."

"What's that?"

"Molly's Christmas turkey and all the leftovers you can carry home."

Chet shook his head. "Well, I suppose I couldn't really ask for anything better than that."

We ate cake while verbally jousting over who'd got the best Christmas present over the years and who'd got the worst clinker. We were all laughing, and second helpings of cake pretty well demolished it to red crumbs.

Jill and I helped Molly clear the table and Mom put on an apron and started running dishwater. Chet was whispering to Al and glancing at us. I suspected a conspiracy of some type and possibly a practical joke. Chet got up, slipped on his boots, and I expected Molly to produce the usual containers of leftovers for him to take home.

Chet pulled on his coat. "Jill and Doug, put on your coats." He walked out the door.

Molly had her arms crossed over her chest. Mom and Al were smiling, so they were onto whatever was about to happen. Jill slipped on her boots and put on her coat. I resigned myself to being a good sport no matter what was being sprung on me.

Chet was standing at the corner of the barn when we came out. He disappeared into the side door and light slipped out onto the snow. I followed Jill in and closed the door. Chet was walking down the center aisle, his boots echoing inside the barn.

He turned to see if we were following. "C'mon. I'm not going to bite you."

Chet stopped in front of a stall and rested his hand on the gate. There were two nearly identical horses in the adjoining stalls, munching hay and looking unconcerned about their visitors.

"I figure since Al's determined to get Doug on a horse, he should have a horse to ride."

I looked into the stalls. "I don't understand."

Jill grabbed my bicep and squeezed. "Chet, you're giving Doug a horse?"

Chet leaned on the gate and looked into the nearest stall. "I'm giving each of you a horse. They're siblings. Turbo is a four-year-old gelding and Misty is a five-year-old mare. Don't let Turbo's name fool you. He's about as docile as a twenty-year-old draft horse." Chet turned to us with tears in his eyes. "Merry Christmas."

Jill threw herself into Chet's arms. "But these are your last two horses."

"I'm done ranching and more comfortable in a pickup than on a horse. It's time for them to have new owners."

I shook Chet's hand. "Thank you."

He slapped my shoulder. "You can thank me by learning to keep your butt in the saddle and thinking about me while you enjoy the view."

Molly met us at the door with a bag for Chet. "We'll be starting to snack at three tomorrow. I'll pull the turkey out about five. Make sure you get over here before the snow starts."

Chet smiled at Molly. "If Al ever throws you out…"

Molly pecked his cheek. "Goodnight Chet."

Al and I shook his hand. Jill and Mom hugged him. Chet held Mom a second longer

162

than Jill and whispered something in her ear. She held his shoulders and looked into his eyes with a big smile, then nodded.

Molly closed the door and Mom said she was going to bed. I intercepted her before she closed the door, afraid Chet had said something that had upset her.

I hugged her. "Goodnight."

"Chet's very special."

"I'm curious about what he whispered to you."

Mom had tears in her eyes. "He said I'd raised you well and that you're the only man he ever felt deserved to be with Jill."

I heard breathing behind me and knew Jill had overheard the conversation. Mom hugged her. "I'm still not entirely convinced Doug's good enough for you."

"Have you been drinking margaritas again?' I joked.

Mom cupped my cheek. "No dear, I'm entirely sober. I wish you two had met twenty-five years ago. But I know Doug wasn't smart enough then to appreciate someone as smart, independent, and spirited as you. I'm glad you've found each other now. And I feel very fortunate to have been accepted by Al and Molly. They've treated me like family."

Mom went into the bedroom and closed the door. Jill hugged me. "We own horses."

"Just how does that work? Do we brand them or license them somehow?"

"Don't be ridiculous. We'll get a bill of sale from Chet and put it away. The bigger issue is boarding them. We'll have to see if Daddy has enough pasture and hay."

"You do know I never wanted a horse."

Jill smiled. "There's an old saying: 'Never look a gift horse in the mouth.'"

"There's another one for dogs, boats, and horses; the cheapest part is the purchase price."

Jill perked up. "Maybe we can buy a pickup and trailer and bring them to Texas."

Her smile said she was kidding, but there was a hint of optimism in her voice. "I don't think the townhouse association would allow us to keep two horses. I'm going to bed."

"Leave the closet light on. I'll be in after I help Mom clean up the kitchen."

Jill must've crept in quietly while I was asleep. I rolled over and threw my arm across her at some point and felt her snuggle into me.

* * *

I smelled coffee and slipped out of bed trying not to wake Jill. It was much easier without the creaking springs in the old mattress set. Al was watching a morning news program with a cup of coffee in his hand, and Molly was draping bacon strips over a huge turkey. The kitchen was already toasty as the oven pre-heated for the bird.

I got a mug out of the cupboard and poured myself a cup of coffee and sidled up to Molly. "Merry Christmas Eve, Mom."

Molly leaned her head on my shoulder. "Merry Christmas to you. Forgive me if I don't hug you with hands that have been pulling giblets out of the turkey."

"That's quite all right. I don't need turkey slime wiped on me. That's a lot of bird."

"We all like leftover turkey."

"You knew Chet was giving us horses for Christmas."

"He mentioned that he was going to have an auction in the spring and didn't want the horses going to some hotshot who wouldn't appreciate them or treat them right. Al might've hinted that they would be welcome here, and Chet came up with the gift plan all on his own."

"The one intended for me is named Turbo. I hope he doesn't live up to his name."

"I'm not the horse person here, so I can't comment one way or the other."

Al overheard us and turned away from the television. "Chet named him that because his sire was a real spitfire. Turbo took after the mare and I think that was a bit disappointing to Chet, but Turbo isn't going to run out from underneath you like his daddy used to do to Chet. If you and Jill are hanging around the house today, we might saddle up the horses and ride the fence line. Has Ronnie ever been on a horse?"

"I don't know."

"Well, maybe she'd like to ride along too."

Mom came walking down the hallway in a robe that looked like a wool serape. "I might like to ride what?"

Al nodded toward the barn. "I told Doug we should take the horses out for a ride today and I was wondering if you'd like to come along."

"I suppose my South Dakota experience would be incomplete without a horse ride."

A kitchen timer chimed, and Molly pulled out a pan of baking powder biscuits. "Everyone grab a chair while the biscuits are hot. I've got sausage gravy, honey, and maple syrup, so we should be able to suit any taste."

I got a mug of coffee for Mom and topped off our mugs while Molly carried a platter of biscuits to the table. Jill wandered into the kitchen as Molly set a big cast iron pan of sausage and gravy on a trivet.

Jill poured herself a mug of coffee. "It's a good thing the kitchen timer woke me, or I assume all the biscuits would be gone."

Al split a pair of biscuits and ladled gravy, full of sausage chunks, over them. "I imagine your mom put another pan in the oven when you walked in the kitchen. She looks out for you."

Ronnie spread butter on a biscuit and then drizzled honey on it. "Molly, you make me feel like I'm on vacation. You're doing all the cooking and cleaning. You barely let me wash dishes."

Al pointed his fork at Molly as she sat down. "Mom's never happier than when she's cooking for a bunch of folks. Ronnie, your being here is a favor. Molly's happy cooking. I'm happy eating. And there's something different to talk about than the weather and politics."

"Hey," Jill said, in mock protest. "Doug and I flew all the way from Texas to be here. Don't we count?"

Molly patted Jill's hand. "Honey, we're pleased as punch that you're here. Ronnie is just icing on the cake."

Ronnie took another biscuit and ladled gravy over it. "I've never eaten biscuits and gravy before." She took a bite and smiled. "Now I see why they're so popular."

Al washed down some biscuit with coffee. "Don't go getting your hopes up that you'll get anything like this at a restaurant. Nobody makes a lighter biscuit or better gravy than Molly."

My phone buzzed and I got up and walked to the hallway while the biscuit discussion went on. "Fletcher."

"Hey, Doug. This is Butch. I thought I'd hold off calling until the end of my shift. I didn't wake you up, did I?"

"No, we were just finishing breakfast. What can I do for you?"

"It's what I can do for you. I've been showing the FBI pictures at the motels, campgrounds, and gas stations all night. One of the all-night gas stations has seen one of the Scorpions. She didn't recognize any of the pictures, but she's seen a guy with the scorpion tattoo on his forearm."

"Was that recently?"

"It was a while ago, probably late summer, but after the Sturgis bike rally. I guess he's probably not the guy you're looking for, but that puts the gang in the area after the Sturgis rally. So, he was here for something besides bike week."

"That's something."

"That's not all. I hit the wall with motels, but I talked to a guy who lives east of town. His neighbor is an Iowan who's only around for a couple weeks in the summer and a week of deer hunting in the fall. The neighbor rents out his cabin the rest of the year through some website. Anyway, the renters have been busy people and some of them were riding in on noisy Harleys until it snowed."

"That sounds like some pretty good police work, Butch. I'll pass that along to my FBI contact. They may want to watch the place to see who's coming and going. They may also want to get the DEA involved."

"I got the name of the owner off a plat map. I thought one of you Feds might want to talk to the owner and see what he can tell you about his renters."

I wrote down the owner's name and address in Ankeny, Iowa. "Thanks, Butch. Go home and get some sleep. I'll call you tonight if I learn anything."

"Say, Fletcher, you're an old cop, right?"

"I retired from the St. Paul police. Why?"

"You know enough to not go riding into that place like the Lone Ranger, right? If these guys are distributing or dealing drugs out there, they'll have an arsenal and won't take kindly to anyone snooping around. They'd probably deal with you like a lot of the ranchers do with the wolves that are illegal to shoot. They use the three 'S' rule: Shoot. Shovel. Shut up."

"That's a good reminder. Thanks."

I punched in Jess Pond's cellphone number. "Merry Christmas, Doug."

"Merry Christmas to you. Say, I shared your photos of the Scorpions with a Custer County deputy. He was poking around on the midnight shift last night and found a gas station clerk who's seen a guy with a scorpion tattoo. He also found someone whose neighbor rented his cabin to a bunch of Harley riders. The neighbor says there's been a lot of traffic in and out of the road and they were riding bikes until the snow hit."

I gave Jess the name and address of the cabin owner, along with Butch's cellphone number.

"Jess, this sounds like more of an FBI, Custer County, and DEA investigation than something related to my murder, so I'm happy to pass this off to you and step away. If you pursue this, please keep my dead camper in mind."

"I'll make some calls and keep you posted."

"I think we're going for a horseback ride, then hunkering down for the blizzard."

"That sounds like a great plan, Doug. You and Jill have a great holiday."

Jill had walked over and caught the end of my conversation. "So, we're done?"

"I guess we'll know more after the FBI looks into the people renting the cabin, but I don't know of anything else we can do right now."

Ronnie twisted around in her chair. "You mean for once you're going to let somebody else lead the posse and you're going to stay home where it's warm and safe?"

I put my hand on her shoulder. "Yes, Mom. Jill and I are not going to get into a gunfight with the bad guys on Christmas Eve."

Al looked disappointed, but Mom said, "Good!"

Chapter Ten

The temperatures had risen ahead of the approaching low-pressure front, so we weren't in danger of immediate frostbite. Mom was excited about going for a ride, so the four of us left Molly with her supper preparations and walked to the barn. Jill showed me how to saddle Turbo and how to tighten the cinch strap.

Turbo was as advertised, a docile, easy-going horse who tolerated my anxiety and inexperience without so much as a dirty look. Al led us through a gate, and we rode a trail onto their former ranch. We were about a mile from the ranch when downy snowflakes started to drift from the clouds.

Jill spurred her horse and got close. "Did I tell you I was eighteen before I knew snowflakes fell from the sky. Until then I thought they just blew in from Wyoming."

I smiled. "It's really that windy all the time?"

"Yup. Pretty much all the time."

On cue, Al turned his horse and stopped next to Mom. They'd been leading us, and now they doubled back.

"We'd best have the horses in the barn and our feet next to the fire before the blow starts."

Our return ride was as leisurely as the ride out. We were all coated with the downy snowflakes that brushed off easily when we got inside the barn. We unsaddled the horses, brushed them, and put hay in their feed troughs.

Chet's pickup was in the driveway and Molly handed us steaming mugs of cider, each with a cinnamon stick, as we hung our coats.

Chet looked me over. "No sign Turbo bucked you off."

"He was as gentle as a lamb." Chet nodded and smiled.

Molly had the table covered with cheese, summer sausage, pickled herring, and crackers. We took our usual chairs and snacked as the wind started to pick up. Molly never sat still. She was fussing with something in a hall closet, then came back to the kitchen carrying two kerosene lanterns and a box of matches. "The power sometimes goes out during these storms and it's best to be prepared."

After an hour of snacking Al stood. "I don't know what Fletchers do for Christmas, but we open presents before we eat turkey on Christmas Eve."

Jill jumped up like a little kid. "Everyone sit down. Doug and I will play Santa and pass out the gifts."

With the gifts distributed, we sat down and Jill looked at the pile in front of her, which happened to be the largest. She was champing at the bit but awaiting the okay to dig into her pile of presents.

Al nodded. "Okay, everyone start."

I sat back and watched as everyone started peeling paper to expose boxes. Jill ripped at her wrapping paper with pieces flying. Molly sat back, watching. She saw me watching Jill and winked at me.

Jill ripped open the boxes of shirts Flora had picked out. She wasn't surprised but seemed pleased. Next came the boots. She paused when she got to the little box. She opened it slowly and carefully took out the earrings. "These are lovely. Thank you."

Ronnie had her boxes open and was admiring her necklace. "What kind of gold is this? I love the pink and green."

Jill held up her earrings. "It's called Black Hills gold. I think you can only find it around here."

Al and Chet held up their matching bottles. Al smiled at me. "I've never been able to afford the good stuff, like this."

Chet got down five lowball glasses and poured an inch of liquor into each of them. He knew I wouldn't partake, but he proudly handed the glasses to Al, Molly, Ronnie, and Jill. He lifted his glass. "Well, this is one heck of a fine Christmas present. Thank you, Jill and Doug."

I opened a box with a western-cut shirt from Al and Molly, and a watch from Jill. Mom gave me a tooled western belt, but I stopped at a flat, heavy box that said it was from Chet.

"You already gave us horses, Chet. You didn't need to give us anything else." I unwrapped the box and opened it. Inside was an antique, black powder pistol with pearl grips. Most of the bluing had been worn away.

"That was my father's. Since I never had any children, and you seem to appreciate guns, I thought you should have it."

I was speechless and nodded my thanks.

Jill opened a smaller flat box. She lifted out a shadow box and stared at it with tears in her eyes. "I can't take this Uncle Chet."

I got up and stood behind her. Inside the shadow box were four silver belt buckles mounted on red felt. I took the box from her hand and read the inscriptions, each an award from a rodeo competition. I looked at Chet for an explanation.

"I won those when I was riding broncs. Didn't seem like much point leaving them on the living room wall. I decided I wanted Jill to have them."

Jill handed the shadow box to me and hugged Chet. "I'll treasure them." She turned to me and explained, "They're the rodeo equivalent of a trophy."

"Makes a lot more sense than an old trophy. At least you can wear a belt buckle."

A kitchen timer rang, and Molly rushed away. I gathered up paper scraps and Jill set the table. The dinner rivaled Thanksgiving and I felt like I was going to pop before Molly handed out pieces of warm apple pie.

A gust of wind made the house shudder, and the lights flickered. Chet looked at the door. "I'd better get going before the roads get too bad."

Molly stopped picking up the wrapping paper. "Nonsense. You stay here tonight. I'll make up the couch for you."

Chet shook his head and got up. "Naw, I'll take my bottle of good booze and go home. If the driving's not too bad I may come back for turkey soup tomorrow."

Molly scooped leftovers into containers Chet had returned earlier and put them into a bag. "This will tide you over until you can get back for soup."

Chet shook our hands, hugged Jill, Mom, and Molly, then put on his wool cap. He untied the earflaps and let them down. "I'll see you tomorrow."

"You call and let us know you made it home," Molly said.

"There ain't no need to do that. I've only got a couple miles to home."

"I don't care. You call."

Chet nodded. The wind blasted in when he opened the door, blowing snowflakes onto the kitchen floor.

Molly watched Chet struggle down the sidewalk. "It's not fit for man nor beast out there, but he's as bullheaded as Al. Once he's decided he's driving home, there's no keeping him here."

Jill joined Molly at the window until Chet's taillights disappeared in the snow.

Mom went back to the table and looked worried. "Chet's not a young man. If he gets stuck, he'll be in real trouble."

Molly found a bottle of sherry in a cabinet. Jill took down glasses and Al poured. I was sipping, and Al was into his second glass when the house was buffeted by another wind gust that made the lights flicker.

Molly got up. "Chet should've called by now." She dialed the phone and listened through many rings.

"Does he have a cellphone?" Mom asked.

"Oh, hell no," Molly replied. "He's just as stubborn as Al. Neither of them will buy a cellphone."

Al nodded. "If you want to talk to me, talk to me. Don't go chasing me down with some electronic gizmo that's like a leash."

Jill got up and nodded toward the door. "Can I take your gelding, Daddy?"

Al nodded and got up. "I'll go with you."

"Daddy, you're in no better shape than Chet. Doug and I will go."

Al glanced at me. "I don't know that Doug's up to this kind of job."

I pulled on my Minnesota Vikings stocking cap and my winter coat. "What's to do? All I have to do is hold the reins and stay in the saddle, right?"

Al grabbed his coat off a peg. "I'll help you saddle up while we negotiate who's going."

I overheard Molly say to Mom in a stage whisper, "That's a first. Al's not known for negotiating anything but the price of cattle."

Just walking to the barn was a struggle. The wind whipped at my coat and blew flakes into my eyes. Al flipped on the lights and pulled blankets and saddles off the railing. Jill brought bridles. I went to Turbo and tightened his cinch strap and checked the stirrups. He seemed totally at ease even though my stomach muscles were clenched, and I was ready to dodge aside if he got restless.

"Why aren't you taking Misty?"

Al led a mottled horse out of a stall. "I'd rather have her on one of our ranch horses, a horse I trust and can rely on."

I nodded, not really sure I understood the issue, but wasn't willing to delve into it more deeply under the circumstances.

Jill led a third horse out of a stall. She saw the question on my face. "This one's for Uncle Chet to ride."

It took two attempts, but I got on Turbo, who seemed unfazed by the rookie on his back. Jill went up on the mottled horse like she'd done a thousand times before. Al put his hand on my thigh and squeezed. "Don't let her out of your sight. If you get separated, just let Turbo have his head and he'll find his way home Do you understand?"

"We'll be okay."

Al opened the barn door and the horses walked into the storm. They seemed less uncomfortable with the driving snow than I was. Jill led the way with the spare horse behind. Turbo seemed to know he should stay close behind the horse in front of him, so I turned up my collar, leaned into the wind, and let him follow.

I couldn't see the road ahead of us and only had an impression we were following the edge of the road. It seemed like we'd been in the saddle for half an hour when Turbo slowed. I could barely make out the massive behind of the horse in front of him and it seemed to be stopped. I tapped Turbo with my heels, and he turned to look at me like I was some kind of fool. I tapped him again and he walked ahead, cutting to the left of the other horse. Jill's saddle was empty, which gave me an adrenaline rush until I looked across the horse and could see just a vague apparition leaning away from me toward the ditch.

Jill stood up and yelled something that was lost in the wind. I shrugged. She put her hand on her horse and tossed the reins to me. Then she brought the third horse ahead. I had no vision of what was going on, but after a minute of commotion I saw Chet's outline in a saddle. Jill took her reins from me. Although we were only two feet apart, I could barely hear her yell, "Follow!"

Turbo knew what was going on and he turned as the other two horses made a U-turn. I assumed we were going back to Rickowski's. I'd never even seen Chet's truck, it being only two horse-widths away, but obscured by the blizzard.

The return trip seemed quicker. I could barely make out the yard light glowing over the barn when Jill jumped off her horse and opened the barn door. The horses didn't need encouragement to enter the warmth and dryness of the barn.

I looked at Jill as she closed the barn door and realized she was encased in snow. I took a glance at Chet and thought he looked like the abominable snowman as he threw his leg over the saddle and dismounted. Turbo snorted and looked at me like I wasn't following the lead. I half-slid, half-fell out of the saddle, not realizing how cold my legs were and how reluctant the muscles were to respond to my commands.

Jill was pulling the bridles off the horses and stringing then up on hooks. "Doug, pull the saddles and blankets off."

I threw saddles over railings like a real cowboy, or how I thought a cowboy might do it. Chet wiped down the horses and Jill led them, one by one into their stalls.

Chet stared at his boots. "I do sincerely apologize. It's a pretty sad day when Al and Molly have to send the kids out to rescue me."

I put my hand on Chet's wet shoulder. "We're hardly kids, and you're not as young as you feel."

Chet looked at me with sudden shock. "Hell, we've got to go back to the truck. I left my bourbon behind the seat." His weathered face grinned. "I was just kidding." He patted his coat. "It's inside my jacket."

We staggered back to the house where Molly, Al, and Mom were gathered around the table looking like they were at a funeral. They all jumped when we opened the door.

Molly rushed to Chet and helped him take off his coat. He held onto his half-empty bottle of booze as if it was gold. Jill and I shook off our coats and pulled off our boots, leaving the entryway covered with melting snow.

Al pulled a handful of lowball glasses down and set them out in front of everyone. "You three look like you could use some antifreeze."

I put up my hand. "Thanks, but I'm adequately thawed."

Jill let Al pour a quarter inch of booze into her glass, then stopped him. She threw it back like a gunslinger at a saloon, then started to cough.

Al smiled for the first time since we walked in the door. "This is smooth sipping whisky, Jill."

"I think someone switched your sipping whisky out for kerosene!"

Molly took a sip, then disappeared down the hallway, returning with a pile of bedding. She spread sheets on the couch and threw a pillow and quilt on top of them. "There you go, Chet. This is what I should've done in the first place."

"I guess I didn't realize it was quite as nasty as it is." Chet nodded to Jill and me. "And I thank you kindly for saving my hide, although you could've waited until morning."

Jill shook her head. "You would've been an icicle by morning."

Chet grabbed the neck of the whisky bottle. "Old Jack would've kept me warm and defrosted until morning."

Molly pushed Chet toward the bathroom. "You strip out of those wet jeans and I'll hang a dry pair on the doorknob for you."

Jill patted her thigh. "Yeah, I think I'll just take these off and go to bed. Cmon, Doug."

Jill closed the bedroom door and threw her arms around me. "Do you feel like a real cowboy?"

I snorted. "Turbo did all the work."

"That's how ranch work is. You train a horse really well, and he does most of the work while your job is to stay in the saddle."

"I doubt that."

"Throw your wet jeans on the floor. I'll take them to the kitchen, and they can drip on the linoleum overnight."

I pulled on flannel pants and carried my jeans to the kitchen. Molly was turning back the corner of the quilt when Chet came out of the bathroom, holding Al's jeans up with one hand. "I guess Al's a little thicker around the middle than I am."

Al waved off his comment. "You're just sucking in your gut to impress the women. We've worn the same size jeans for seventy years."

Jill leaned close. "I think Uncle Chet will be okay. He's back to needling Daddy."

"You were worried?" I whispered.

"Goodnight everyone," Jill said with a wave. She grabbed my hand and led me to the bedroom. She closed the door and leaned against it. "Chet's teeth were chattering when I opened his pickup door. His engine died when he went into the ditch and he would've died if we hadn't gone out with the horses."

"He and your dad aren't young men anymore."

"But they don't know it. They're just bullheaded…"

I pulled her into my arms. "They're okay. They're just getting old and haven't accepted it yet."

"Yes, they have. Daddy sold off most of his ranch and Uncle Chet is leasing his land."

I nodded. "They see the handwriting on the wall."

"Have you noticed Mom? She's up before dawn every day, and she looks more tired every day. She's getting old, too. We're wearing her out."

"But she won't let any of us help."

Jill shook her head. "No, she won't." Jill leaned into me and buried her face in my shoulder. "We should move back and take care of them."

"No, they have their own lives, and they wouldn't tolerate our interference."

"How'd you get so smart, Fletcher?"

"I guess it comes from being a cynical cop. I've seen a hundred cases where adult children have tried to take over their parent's lives. It doesn't work. Period."

"But..."

I put my finger to her lips. "We'll live our lives, and they'll live their lives. Some day we'll get a call from them, or one of their friends, asking for our help. Until then, we do nothing."

My phone buzzed and I struggled to find it among the things I'd emptied from my pockets onto the nightstand. "Fletcher."

"Merry Christmas, Doug."

I looked at the caller ID and saw Jess Pond's name. "Merry Christmas, again, Jess. What's up?"

"The stolen card got used again tonight."

"At another ATM?"

"Our guy must've been testing it out at the ATMs to see if it had been cancelled. He must be confident we're not onto him because he used it to book three motel rooms."

"Where?"

"Down the road from you, in Spearfish."

"I hate to tell you this, Jess, but we just went out on horseback to rescue Jill's neighbor. We're not going to Spearfish any time soon."

"And all the roads and the interstate are closed, so our guy isn't going anywhere either."

"So, what's your plan?"

"I called the sheriff and explained what's been going on. He pulled his patrols off the roads tonight, but once he gets his emergency systems up and running, he's going to get someone into the motel and try to see what our guy looks like and maybe see what he's up to."

"So, he's got people coming down from Custer?"

"Spearfish is in Lawrence County. The county seat is in Lead."

"Jess, this guy is like that whack-a-mole game. Every time we think we might have him he pops up in a different jurisdiction."

"He might be smart enough to keep moving among cities and counties to keep the police off his back. I'll have my people coordinate with all the counties and local police, so he doesn't slip through the cracks."

"You're pulling your people in on Christmas?"

"Like I said, he's not going anywhere until the roads open."

The lights flickered, then went out. "We just lost our lights."

"I hope you get power before the pipes freeze."

"Yeah, Merry Christmas to you, too."

Jess laughed. "Most ranchers have a generator in the barn. You'll be okay."

"Oh, goody! I get to help Dad pull out the generator and get it started."

"Quit whining, Doug. You've been living in the big city too long. By the way, the pump goes out with the electricity, so you don't have water either."

"You're just full of good news, Jess."

I shut down the call and turned off the phone to conserve the battery.

Jill was under the covers. "Jess has something going on in Spearfish?"

I slipped into bed. "The dead camper's credit card was used to rent rooms at a Spearfish motel. Jess is going to coordinate with the sheriff to see if they can get a picture of the guy and see what he's up to."

"After the roads open."

"Right. After the roads open. Does your dad have a generator?"

"He used to. I suppose it's in the garage or barn. You can help him get it going in the morning if the power's not back on before then."

"How would the power come back before then if the roads are closed and the power company trucks can't get to the downed lines?"

"Good point. Snuggle close. It'll be cold by morning."

Chapter Eleven

I awoke to the sound of feet shuffling around the kitchen. Jill's arm was draped over me and her body was spooned against my back. My face, the only part of me outside a quilt, was cold. I was reminded of Boy Scout winter camping experiences in Minnesota. I'd been awarded a Zero Hero badge for spending an entire weekend outside in below zero temperatures. I'd resolved to never do that again, at least not willingly.

I wiggled out from under the quilt and Jill quickly scooted into the warm space I'd vacated.

"You don't have to get up yet. Daddy will get the heaters and generator going."

I pulled on a thermal t-shirt and long underwear, then added layers of jeans, flannel shirts, fleece, and a down vest. Jill resigned herself to the fact that I wasn't generating my share of body heat anymore and she crawled out of bed and slipped on clothes under her long flannel nightshirt.

I smelled coffee and saw dim, yellow light in the kitchen. Molly had a ceramic pot heating on the gas stove and was quietly mixing something in a bowl with a giant wooden spoon. I was about to say something when she nodded toward the living room. Chet was asleep, leaning against the arm of the couch. His arm was draped over Mom's shoulders, her head was on his chest, and they were under many layers of quilts.

Molly was smiling and put her finger to her lips. I heard the scraping of a shovel outside, then the barn door creaked. I assumed Al was already tending to the horses or trying to start a generator. I put on my coat, pulled on the Vikings stocking cap, and opened the door. It was still dark out, only days past the winter solstice, but the blizzard wind had lessened, and I could see stars. A gust of wind stirred a tiny tornado of snow near the barn.

The inside of the barn was warm and smelled of hay, wet leather, and horses. A light from a lantern led me to an alcove on the far side of the building. Al was pouring fuel into the tank of a large generator. I startled him when I walked into the area lit by the kerosene lantern.

"Can I help?"

Al flipped a switch on the side of the generator. "Well, this is either going to start or not. Let's hope for the best." He pushed a button and the generator cranked over slowly, then fired and ran. The barn lights came on and Al smiled.

"Looks like success to me."

Al picked up the lamp and turned the handle to retract the wick until the light died.

"Let's go inside. It'll warm up pretty quickly now there's power to the furnace."

"Do we need to do anything with the horses?"

"I gave them some hay before I messed with the generator." He paused in the aisle between the horse stalls. "A good rancher knows electricity is nice but taking care of your horses is a necessity."

We entered the house. When Al closed the door, Chet's head popped up. He realized Mom was leaning against him and he pulled his arm back like he'd been burned. His face turned bright red, then he gently put his arm back on Mom's shoulders, then she let out a contented murmur.

Al saw that play out and one corner of his mouth curled. "Nothing wrong with sharing body heat when it's cold," he said to me in a whisper.

I nodded. Chet looked like he expected me to cause a scene. I disabused that notion by smiling, then going to the cupboard and taking down mugs.

Jill joined us at the table and Molly poured coffee from the ceramic pot. "There will be coffee grounds at the bottom, so don't drink your cup empty. I'll have some pancakes on the griddle in a bit."

The hot coffee, made by boiling the grounds directly in the water, was strong, but gave me warmth. Bacon started sizzling in a pan, and Molly gave the batter a last stir before ladling it onto the griddle.

Mom stirred, reacting to the sound and smell of frying bacon. Her eyes opened and she sat up, assessing the unfamiliar surroundings. She looked at Chet, who had two days beard and hair that looked like he'd stirred, rather than combed it, then she leaned back with her head on his chest. Chet had his arm in the air, not quite sure where to put it. He rested it on the back of the sofa, then looked at us. We all smiled and the red slowly faded from his face.

Mom's eyes opened, and she looked at Chet's arm. She reached out from under the quilt and pulled it around her, which made Chet blush yet again. Then she closed her eyes and smiled.

I was finishing my pancakes and drinking my third cup of coffee when Mom pulled a quilt around herself and stood up. She walked to the table, leaving Chet scrambling to cover the long underwear he'd been sleeping in. He scurried to the bathroom with the borrowed jeans in one hand and his shirt in the other.

Molly poured the last of the coffee from the ceramic pot into Mom's mug while the electric coffee maker gurgled on the counter. "Are you ready for bacon and pancakes, Ronnie?"

"That sounds great." She took a sip of coffee, then looked at the ceiling light fixture. "When did the power come back on?"

"Al started the generator about twenty minutes ago."

Mom nodded, then realized we were all staring at her. "What?"

I smiled and glanced at the couch.

"I got cold and I figured I could either crawl in bed with you two or come out here and keep Chet warm."

Jill nodded. "It would've been cozy with three of us in my bed."

Chet came out of the bathroom carrying the quilt. He folded it and set it neatly on the wrinkled sheets. He nodded at the rest of us but shied away from Mom.

"Thanks for sharing your body heat, Chet. I was chilled to the bone."

Chet glanced at her and nodded, blushing again.

Mom set down her coffee. "Let me set the record straight. I was cold. Chet and I shared our blankets and slept on the couch. Chet was a perfect gentleman."

Chet looked relieved and smiled at Mom. Then he nodded.

Mom smiled back, and although nothing physical happened, I thought a milestone had passed in the cold darkness of the living room. Jill must've sensed the same thing because she reached under the table and squeezed my knee.

Al broke the spell by announcing that the three men were going to Chet's pickup to pull it out of the ditch. My first thought was that a tow truck would be more efficient. But Chet agreed that a tractor and chains would work just fine.

They're rugged independent people who rely on each other, I thought.

Molly set plates of bacon and pancakes in front of Chet and Mom. "I almost forgot, Merry Christmas!"

I saw Jill freeze as her eyes went wide. "Hang on. I forgot a present!"

She went into the bedroom and came back with a package and handed it to Molly. "I had this tucked away so I wouldn't lose it, then I forgot about it in the excitement of last night."

Molly rolled the elongated rectangular package in her hands and read the label. "This is from Jill and Doug."

She carefully peeled the wrapping paper off as if she planned to reuse it, unlike Jill who'd ripped and shredded her way into every package as if she couldn't wait a second to see what was inside. Molly folded the paper, set in on the table, and examined the box before gently lifting the lid.

Al couldn't stand the slow revelation. "What is it?"

She set the box on the table and lifted out the gift with both hands. "It's a bracelet."

Jill stood up and walked behind her. "They're alternating diamonds and sapphires. Doug's April birthstone is a diamond and mine's a sapphire."

Molly draped the bracelet over her wrist and let Jill fasten it. Molly looked at me with glistening eyes. "I know I asked for something with your birthstones, but…"

Jill hugged Molly from behind. "Merry Christmas, Mom."

All of us were silent until Al looked at Chet and smiled. "And I thought our booze cost a lot!"

I bumped elbows with Al. "Don't you think she's worth it?"

That had Al tongue tied, but Chet replied, "She's worth that and more. Maybe I'll buy her one next year with my birthstone."

Mom laughed. "What's your birthstone, Chet?"

"I don't rightly know."

"When's your birthday?"

"I'm a leap year baby," Chet said with a smile. "I'm only seventeen."

Molly laughed. "Well, you certainly act like you're seventeen sometimes."

Jill and I cleared the table. Mom went to her bedroom to get dressed. Al went to the barn to check on the generator, while Molly and Chet chatted at the table.

"What are we going to do to celebrate Christmas Day?" Jill asked.

"What did we do when you were a little girl and we got snowbound?" Molly asked.

Jill stood by the counter and thought. "We'd do jigsaw puzzles."

Molly pointed to the hallway. "Doug, look on the top shelf of the hallway closet."

I had to stand on my toes to reach the dusty boxes on the top shelf. I set them on the table, and Jill grabbed a dust rag from under the sink.

"Looks like a map of the United States—and look at this note at the bottom. 'Now including Hawaii and Alaska!'"

Jill pulled out a second box. "I remember this. It's zoo animals. And the next one is faces of the presidents."

"Who's the last president?" I asked.

Molly shook her head. "Dwight Eisenhower."

We dumped out the United States puzzle and spread the pieces on the table as Mom came out of the bedroom with her hair freshly brushed. "I haven't done a jigsaw puzzle in forever. How fun!"

Molly pulled edge pieces to the side of the table. "There aren't a lot of things you can do by kerosene lamp, and this was how we kept busy while we waited for the road to get plowed."

Chet pulled out two corner pieces. "This is the top, left corner. See how it has a little of Alaska on it. Junior pointed that out to me the first time we did this puzzle."

The room went silent and we pretended not to notice the elephant Chet had just brought into the room.

Mom looked at us all, confused. "Who's Junior?"

When no one spoke, I said, "Jill had a twin brother, Al junior. He died in a ranch accident when they were teenagers."

Chet was trying to backpedal. "I didn't mean to…"

Molly waved him off. "Junior's been dead and buried for over thirty years. Jill's home for Christmas and I have a new son-in-law. We gained a new relative, Ronnie, who's delightful, and there's a new year just around the corner."

Chet nodded. "We've got a lot to be thankful for." He paused. Molly, I'd take a cup of eggnog with a dollop of that good whisky."

Molly got up and walked to the refrigerator. "I'll pour eggnog, but don't you think it's a little early to start the whisky?"

"Well, it's Christmas, and I thought a touch of Jack might get the taste of boot out of my mouth."

That broke the ice and we laughed. Mom got up to help Molly. "I might take a dollop of Jack in my eggnog too."

I walked to the bedroom while the others worked the jigsaw puzzle and punched Jess Pond's number into my cellphone. "Merry Christmas, Jess."

"Merry Christmas to you, too. Do you have power out there in the country?"

"Only because my father-in-law has a generator. We went out on horseback last night to rescue a neighbor who'd gone into the ditch. I'm having lots of new ranch experiences."

"I suppose you're calling about our biker in the motel."

"Do you know anything new?"

"One of my agents rode to the hotel this morning on a snowmobile. He claimed to be a good Samaritan seeing if there was anyone with an emergency situation. The interstate closure has all the motels, truck stops, and school gymnasiums jammed with people, so no one who has a room is going anywhere. The agent spoke with the desk clerk, then checked on the people who were in the breakfast nook eating waffles and drinking coffee. Our biker was at a corner table with two women. My agent took a cellphone picture of them. The man's face shows up in some of the gang pictures from Denver. The two women he was with were…he said they looked like they'd been ridden hard and put away wet."

"Did the biker have a scorpion tattoo?"

"We can't tell. He was wearing a black long-sleeve shirt and black driving gloves. The agent didn't hang around because he said this biker was eyeing everyone in the breakfast room like he was extremely paranoid."

"Do you have any idea when the roads will open up?"

"The governor has called out the National Guard to rescue people stranded on the interstate. I assume the plows will be out today. They may get a single lane opened up for emergency vehicles, but there's a travel ban and realistically, it's going to be two days before people can dig out their cars and start driving around again. Besides, there won't be any stores open to drive to because none of the workers can get to their jobs. The hotel was holding three rooms and they had their staff sharing the rooms and sleeping in rotating in twelve-hour shifts."

"So, what's your plan, Jess?"

"I've been on the phone with Custer and Lawrence Counties, as well as the South Dakota Highway Patrol and the highway department. As soon as I can mobilize people, we're going to set up an operation in the motel to arrest the biker."

"How about the women with him?"

"I've got an agent cruising the internet to see if they're advertising outcall massage or escort services. We've got their pictures, and we'll compare them to the faces he finds on the internet."

I closed my eyes. "There are outcall escorts and massage available here, in the middle of the Black Hills?"

"Doug, don't be naïve. There are working girls everywhere there's a guy who's willing to pay for sex."

"This feels like a small town."

"Just because you're in a small town, doesn't mean there's not someone who's willing to pay for an hour of pleasure, and someone who's willing to provide it."

"I guess."

I went back to the kitchen where Al had joined the jigsaw puzzle team. Jill walked over and caught me in the hallway. "I assume you were on the phone with Jess."

I told her about my conversation and the gridlock the blizzard had caused. "We'd might as well enjoy the jigsaw puzzles."

* * *

The rumble of a snow plow caught everyone's attention. Al went to the window and nodded. "Harry just turned around in the yard. We can dig out our pickups and get ready to pull Chet out of the ditch."

Molly shook her head. "There's nowhere to go, so you don't need to rush."

Al made a face. "I'd like to pull Chet's truck out while it's daylight."

Molly looked over her shoulder. "There'll be daylight again tomorrow."

Chet glanced at Molly, Al, and Mom. "Well, I should probably try to sleep in my own bed tonight rather than imposing on your hospitality again."

Molly shook her head. "Chet, no one else is using that couch tonight. You'd might as well stay. Besides, you'd just turn around and be back here tomorrow morning anyway."

"Naw, I'd hang around my own house."

Jill put her hand on Chet's shoulder. "Why do that when you've got family here?"

Chet looked at her. "I thank you kindly." Then he looked at Molly. "Well, if it's not too much bother."

Molly made a shushing sound. "It's no bother at all. The couch is already made up and

I've got plenty of food for everyone. Besides, there's no power at your house. You'd best stay here where it's warm and light."

Chet nodded, then glanced at Mom. "You don't mind having a stranger around the house?"

"Like Molly said, you're family. If anyone's a stranger, it's me."

Al brought a handful of lowball glasses to the table and brought Chet's bottle of Gentleman Jack to the table. "Since we're not going to pull out Chet's truck, I'm declaring happy hour."

I smiled. "You're drinking Chet's whisky?"

"It seems kind of silly to open a second bottle. Chet and I both know that the only ones drinking this good booze are sitting at this table. When his is gone, we'll finish off mine."

I looked at Chet who nodded.

* * *

Jill and I took a break mid-afternoon and shoveled the snow away from the pickups in the yard. We'd assembled all three puzzles through the afternoon and evening. Molly made soup from the turkey carcass and made buns for supper. Al added fuel to the generator to keep the furnace running through the night. Jill and I claimed exhaustion and went to bed at nine while the others sat around the table sipping sherry.

I changed into flannel sleep pants. "Where do you think my Mom will be sleeping in the morning?"

Jill modestly slipped a flannel nightshirt over her head and stripped off her clothes from underneath it. "She'll be in bed and Chet will be on the couch. Last night was cold and they were just sharing body heat on the couch."

"I saw some wayward glances that made me thing Chet may have found second base under the sheet."

Jill crawled under the sheet and glared at me. "Really? They just met."

"There's nothing wrong with anything that happens. They're both lonely people."

Jill rolled away from me. "Go to sleep."

I spooned with her and put my hand on her flat stomach. "The bed doesn't squeak."

"Down boy. There are four people on the other side of the door."

"It's Christmas."

Jill rolled over and faced me. "Are you trying to make up for lost time?"

"I told Rachel to cherish every day as if it were her last."

Jill touched my cheek. "I do cherish every day."

"Well?"

"Just because I'm cherishing every day, doesn't mean I want to have sex every night."

"We didn't last night. So, it's not every night. And today's a holiday."

"You told me you'd want to hold me every night even if you could never have sex again."

"That's true. But I think you can tell that I'm still able to perform."

Jill pushed her pelvis against mine and kissed me. "You're incorrigible."

"That's a polite way of putting it."

Chapter Twelve

I heard bedsprings squeak after everyone went to bed, then again early, before anyone was up. I wondered if it was my mother making bathroom trips, or if she'd had a visitor. I hoped it was the latter. Both she and Chet deserved some moments of tenderness, even if she was flying back to St. Paul when the airport reopened.

I beat everyone, even Molly, to the kitchen and started coffee. Then I jumped in the shower and shaved. Molly was pulling down coffee mugs when I walked into the kitchen.

"I'm sorry if I woke you up when I showered," I said.

"I was awake, just not ready to get out of bed yet."

I'd just sipped my coffee when my phone buzzed. "Fletcher," I said as I walked into the hallway.

"Are the roads open by you yet?" Jess Pond asked.

"The plow came through yesterday afternoon and we dug the pickups out after that. What's up?"

"Can you meet us behind the Spearfish truck stop at ten o'clock?"

I walked into the bedroom as Jill was making the bed. "Sure, we can be at the truck stop at ten. What's going on?"

I turned on the speakerphone so Jill could hear. "Our internet guy found a website used by people who are looking for extramarital…encounters. He found posts from the two women who were with the biker."

"So, what's the plan?"

"The Lawrence County sheriff wants to set up a prostitution sting."

"Sounds good. You're going to let us observe?"

"Actually, the sheriff is concerned that all his deputies are recognizable. They need someone who looks like a middle-aged married trucker to act as the John."

Jill's eyes narrowed. "Jess, this is Jill. Doug isn't going to have sex with some crack whore so you can arrest her."

Jess laughed. "The Johns don't actually have sex with the girls. They entice them into agreeing to a price for some services. We have a microphone to record the agreement. Our John says some code phrase, the cops burst into the room and make the arrest before anyone gets naked."

Jill was shaking her head. "Uh uh. No way Doug is going into that situation. This has nothing to do with the National Park Service.

It's not our bust, it's not our job, it's not our jurisdiction."

"I already spoke with the regional National Park Service office and they've given permission for you and Doug to assist."

I leaned back and let Jill vent. "I don't like this, Jess."

"There's nothing to it. We do a seven 'P' operation. Proper prior planning prevents piss poor performance. The whole thing will be orchestrated, and we'll have lots of backup from Lawrence County and the South Dakota Highway Patrol."

Jill looked at me, but asked Jess, "And there's nothing that can go wrong?"

"Well, there's always a chance there will be a surprise, but Doug's a seasoned cop and we'll have people right outside the door. If something goes south, we'll have plenty of people to deal with it."

"And I'll be right there beside them."

"I thought we'd have you listen in from the control center."

"That was a statement, Jess, not a question. And I'll be right there."

Jess paused. "There'll be a ton of people in heavy body armor on the entry team."

"Damnit, Jess, you're not giving me warm fuzzies here. You'll have people in heavy body armor and Doug will have what, a microphone and his good looks."

"Listen Jill, there are thousands of prostitution busts a year and nothing happens.

We'll have overwhelming force on the other side of the motel door. There won't be two seconds between Doug giving the code word and half a dozen heavily armed cops rushing in and screaming. It's bullet proof."

"Yeah, but Doug's not. I'm on the entry team or we stay at the ranch until you tell us the party is over."

Jess sighed. "Okay, but I want you in body armor."

"I brought a soft vest."

"I'll have a heavy vest for you, Jill. One that'll stop a rifle bullet."

Jill looked at me and was mouthing, "No."

I muted the phone. "This may get us the girl who was with the dead guy. Maybe we'll find out what happened to him."

I unmuted the phone. "We'll be there at ten, Jess."

I shut down the phone and Jill stuck me in the chest with her finger. "This is *not* the wild west, and you are *not* the Lone Ranger. Got it?" She paused, then added, "And don't say, 'yes dear' because I'm not kidding around here. This is serious, and I'm dead serious. I'm not going to be a widow this afternoon."

I pulled her close. "You're not going to be a widow this afternoon. But I'd rather have you listening in from the command post."

"This is not negotiable. Either I'm with the entry team, or we're staying here and putting together puzzles. Which is it?"

"You're on the entry team. But you're going to have to explain this to our parents."

Jill explained that we had to go to Spearfish for the investigation and somehow glossed over the part that I was to be the bait in a prostitution sting, and she would be wearing a bullet-proof vest capable of stopping a rifle bullet as part of the team busting into the motel room with guns drawn.

The National Park Service pickup truck wasn't pleased about starting even though the wind was calm, and the temperature had risen to zero Fahrenheit. I had to remind myself that although I had four-wheel-drive this truck wouldn't stop any faster than any other vehicle. I'd been told by a former St. Paul police partner that four-wheel-drive just meant you'd get stuck further in the ditch than the other vehicles. We passed Chet's truck in the ditch and it looked like it would take a lot more than a tractor and chain to get it out from under the snow that had been pushed over it by the plow.

Jill spent the drive looking silently out the side window at the white landscape marred only by fence posts and the top strand of barbed wire.

"What's going through your mind?"

"I'm scared."

"Every good cop is scared going into an operation. That helps you stay focused and able to react. It's the people who aren't scared that I worry about. They're either cocky, which makes them dangerous, or they aren't smart enough to know when they're in danger."

205

"Remember the barn in Hulett. The sheriff and FBI had that all planned and it went to pieces. They were going to arrest that guy and he ended up dead in his wife's arms on the back steps."

Jill glossed over her role in his death, probably compartmentalizing it to help her stay sane.

"This will be easy. There'll be a half-naked woman crying with four cops pointing guns at her. These prostitution stings are nothing to worry about."

"Yeah, where's the biker going to be?"

I paused, knowing she'd seen the wild card in the deck. "I'm sure they'll have him isolated somewhere and will take him down at the same time they grab the girl."

"How can you be sure of that?"

"The odds are ninety-nine percent that he'll be in cuffs the same time the woman gets cuffed. All you and I will do is stand back and stay out of the way."

"You sound so confident."

"Jess said it well, proper prior planning prevents piss poor performance. It's the 'Seven-P' plan. The FBI is known for planning operations to the point of boredom."

Jill looked out the side window. "They were in on the Hulett plan, too."

"Not everything goes as planned every time."

"That's why I'm scared. I know how terribly wrong things can go."

About a mile from the motel, we saw the group of police vehicles gathered behind the truck stop. Jess stepped out of the back of a panel van as we pulled up. There were three deputies, a highway patrolman and two FBI agents gathered around, drinking coffee. The spot was somewhat sheltered from the wind, steam rising from Styrofoam coffee cups.

A young female FBI agent smiled at Jill. "I hear your husband is going to be the bait. I'm happy to be on the entry team instead of 'the college kid making the drug buy' for a change."

"You've done this before?"

"Dozens of times. I'm out of that job now. All the dealers in the area have seen my face too many times."

The Lawrence County sheriff came out of the truck stop carrying a carton of coffee cups. He handed Jill and I each a cup and introduced himself as Rick Wilson. He was tall, with a long face. His head was covered by a "Rocky the squirrel" hat, the earflaps down.

Jess took me into the back of the van, grabbed the pull tab on my jacket's zipper and attached a loop and tag from a local ski resort. I recognized the tag as the "lift ticket" that identified the wearer as having paid for use of the lift. They were on jackets all over ski areas.

"The microphone is inside the paper tag. The code phrase is 'Mickey Mouse.' You tell the hooker whatever she's doing is Mickey

Mouse and we fly through the door. Now say 'Mickey Mouse' to make sure the bug picks up your voice."

I said the words and heard my voice echo back in a slightly higher pitch a fraction of a second later. A technician sitting at the receiver console gave me a thumbs up.

"Now, give me your cellphone."

"Why?"

"We're going to send a text to the number in the advertisement. She'll want a selfie so she will recognize your face through the peephole in the door."

"Ah, I'm not sure that's something that'll fly with the National Park Service. It's a government phone and I'm sure there's some regulation about using it for sending selfies to hookers."

Jess smiled, took my phone, and handed it to the guy operating the radio. Without needing my passcode, he somehow accessed my account and sent a text. A response came less than a minute later.

He passed the phone back. "Go outside and take a selfie. Make sure there aren't any cops or police cars in the background. If you happen to get a semi in the picture the hooker might assume you're a trucker and that would be okay."

I walked behind the truck stop, faced away from the police vehicles, and took a picture that I sent as part of the text string now on my phone.

"Room 218." Came back.

My mind raced and although we hadn't discussed it, I sent a return text.

"Picture of you?"

There was a long pause, then my phone chimed. A picture, obviously taken inside a motel room, showed up. The woman tried to have a lascivious look, but it came off as pouty. She was wearing a tight tank top that exposed cleavage. There was nothing visible below her breasts, so I had no idea if her arms were covered with needle tracks, if she had tattoos, or if she was holding a gun. I felt queasy.

I walked back to Jess and the sheriff. "She texted me that she's in room 218. Do you know where her boyfriend is?"

"He rented three rooms, which really pissed off the night clerk when they closed the interstate. They were trying to get everyone to double up and the biker told him no. Your date's in the middle of his three rooms: 216 218, 220. The other hooker is in 216 with a customer, and the biker's in 220. We'll take him at the same time we come into your room. We'll get the other woman later."

Jill joined us after talking with the female FBI agent. "This isn't just a prostitution sting."

Jess looked at the sheriff. "No. We have intel that they're dealing meth and speed, too."

"How many guns?"

"The guy is sitting on a pile of cash he collects from the women after every transaction. I'm sure he's got some firepower in the cash room, but we don't think he'd let the women have guns."

"Aren't you afraid some civilian is going to get hurt?" Jill asked.

"Everyone's been checking out and we've got most of the floor clear. We've got the housekeeping people downstairs in the laundry."

The sheriff looked at me. "You'd better get going. If you're not there in another couple minutes she's going to book another customer." He held out his hand. "Let me hold your weapon, badge, and ID until afterwards."

I unclipped the holster and badge from my belt and handed him my wallet. In return he handed me a folded wad of bills. "She'll want to see the cash, but don't go for the first price she throws out or she'll suspect you're a cop."

A Lawrence County deputy was sitting in a red pickup idling beside us. "Gus is going to drive you over in his pickup. We'll come around the back and get up to the room. As soon as you agree on the price, you say the code phrase and we rush in."

Jess handed Jill an FBI vest with a breastplate that looked like it was an inch thick. She was adjusting the Velcro straps when Gus drove me to the hotel.

I was nearly knocked over by the wind when I stepped out of the pickup. Gus smiled at me and said, "Micky Mouse."

The motel lobby had three people talking with the desk clerk. The clerk looked at me quizzically but didn't acknowledge me as a cop or question me. The second floor seemed deserted, no noise coming from any room I passed.

I knocked on room 218 and heard shuffling behind the door. The peephole went dark as my "date" checked me out. The chain slid on the back of the door and the bolt clicked. The woman staring at me was close to forty but was trying hard to look eighteen. She wore a lot of makeup and her bleached hair was tied in a ponytail. The tank top I'd seen in her selfie was a size too small to accommodate her surgically enhanced breasts, and her very short shorts exposed thighs so thin I was surprised she could walk up the stairs unaided. She smiled exposing teeth that looked well past the aid of a dentist, probably due to meth use.

Her voice was husky, like a heavy smoker. "Hi, honey. C'mon in."

I wanted to run screaming down the hall but suppressed the urge and walked in the room. The bedspread was thrown haphazardly on the bed and the pillows were at odd angles, probably due to activities I didn't want to dwell on. There was an unlabeled pill bottle on the nightstand along with some packets containing white powder. She reached for my jacket zipper and I wanted to slap her hand away but braced myself and let her pull it down in a move she tried to make seductive.

"I haven't had a lot of luck with this site," I said. "You're the first response I've had. I thought we could get something to eat and get to know each other."

She ran her hand over my shoulders, pushing my jacket over my arms. "You don't need to buy me a meal," she purred. "I'd prefer cash."

I tried to look surprised. "I thought this was a dating site."

"I'm an escort if that's what you're looking for. I'm not free."

"What's the going rate?"

She cocked her head. "Depends on your appetite. There are things that I can do with my clothes on, or there are more expensive things that'll take a little longer and cost you a little more."

I reached for my coat, thinking I might just walk away and let the sheriff find another John, then remembering Rick's admonition to negotiate so I didn't look like a cop. "I'm out of here."

She laid her hand on my chest. "You don't have to rush off."

"I thought I was going on a date."

"How much did you think you were going to spend on a couple drinks and a steak? We can probably work something out for that."

She started unbuttoning my shirt, which gave me goosebumps. She took that as enthusiasm, and she stepped back to pull off her tank top.

"I'm serious. I'm leaving."

She unbuttoned the top of her shorts but stopped short of pulling the zipper.

"Oh, I don't think you want to leave before I make you happy."

"Like I said, I don't have a lot of cash."

"You were probably going to drop a hundred bucks on a cheating wife who might not put out and if she had, she wouldn't have made you half as happy as I'll make you."

"So, you're going to make me happy for a hundred dollars?"

"I'll make you a lot happier for two hundred."

"This is a pretty Mickey Mouse set up," I said, looking at my coat on the floor.

I expected people to come rushing through the door, but nothing happened. The hooker slid her shorts over her slender hips. I kept eye contact with her, not wanting to know what she was, or wasn't wearing under her shorts."

This time I spoke louder. "I said this was Mickey Mouse."

Again, nothing happened at the door. The hooker stepped toward me, reaching for my belt and I nearly ran to the window and unlatched it. Her hands were on my back.

"You need a little air, honey?"

I slammed the heel of my hand into the window frame to break it free of the frost. I slid it open and stuck my head out and yelled, "Will someone tell Mickey Mouse it's show time?"

Gus, the deputy who'd dropped me off, was standing next to the motel entrance. He was so shocked to see my head sticking out of the window that he nearly fell on the packed snow. "Micky Mouse!" he yelled into his shoulder mounted radio.

Instead of the hallway door flying open and a half dozen cops rushing in, the door connecting to the adjacent room slammed into the wall next to my shoulder. The biker burst in, looking like a raging bull. "What the hell is going on?"

The hooker recoiled and pointed at me. "He keeps yelling Mickey Mouse. He's nuts!"

I heard a key card slip in the door as the biker threw a punch at me. I ducked the roundhouse he'd thrown, but I had nothing to protect myself but my hands, and I was sure he'd been in a lot more bar fights than I had. I stumbled back and grabbed a lamp off the nightstand, holding it in front of me as he swung his arm overhand, like he was planning a Karate chop.

The lamp shattered under his blow. A half dozen voices yelling "POLICE!" screamed behind him. He spun and lashed out at the first cop.

Though it looked like he was going to slap the cop, there was no smacking sound and the cop screamed. More cops rushed in with guns drawn, but they hesitated because the biker had no obvious weapons. Looking at the first cop who'd been knocked to the floor, I saw the side of his face was covered with blood running from a wound on his neck.

"He's got a knife inside his glove!" I yelled.

The deputies seemed oblivious to my shout and a second man reached out to grab the biker's arm. In a flash the biker slashed the deputy's forearm deeply, garnering a scream.

I'd become attuned to Jill's voice and even among the screams of pain and "Police" I heard her yell, "Get down!"

Dropping to the floor, I was deafened by a series of gunshots. My ears were ringing, and someone was screaming into a radio for an ambulance. I pulled a pillowcase off a pillow and held it to the wounded deputy's neck. He looked at me in shock, not realizing he was bleeding heavily through the gash in his neck.

Jill was screaming at me although the words were lost in the chaos. She straddled the biker as more people rushed into the room. Rick, the sheriff, took in the scene and was on his radio calling for rescue crews and multiple ambulances. An FBI agent ripped the bedspread off the bed and threw it at the naked hooker. Then he pulled off the top sheet and made it into a compress, pushing me aside and pressing it to the neck of the deputy I'd been helping.

I stood and looked at Jill, who was straddling the biker, her gun trained on him as his body spasmed and he gurgled. With the pool of his blood spreading quickly, I knew he wouldn't last until an ambulance arrived. Jill's eyes were fixed on my bloody hands.

I finally heard Jill speaking in clipped phrases. "Are you deaf? I've been asking if you're okay!"

"I'm fine."

The biker's body stopped moving. A moment later he exhaled in a gurgling rattle. I reached down and tried to pull the biker's glove off, to remove the knife from his hand. I struggled and realized the glove covered some sort of prosthesis. I finally got the glove free and looked at the four metal fingers, each sharpened to a point, like lion's claws.

It took Jill a moment to process what she was seeing, then her eyes went wide. "He killed the hiker. He ripped the guy's throat open."

I nodded.

Jess stepped behind Jill and touched her shoulder. "I need you to holster your weapon and step into the hallway while we process this crime scene."

I guided Jill into the hallway where the female FBI agent was talking to the hooker now wrapped in the bedspread. Farther down the hall, the sheriff was talking to a younger redheaded woman who was wearing nothing but a hoodie that reached to her hips.

I took Jill's arm and steered her toward the stairs, then took her into my arms. The adrenaline faded quickly, and she began to shake, and then sob. We stepped aside as two paramedics ran down the hallway, responding to a deputy who was waving them into the scene of the shooting. Two firemen followed with more rescue gear and a second set of EMTs pushed a gurney out of the elevator and ran down the hallway with it.

Jill leaned against the wall and slid down until she was sitting with her elbows on her knees.

I sat next to her. "You did good."

"Bullshit. I shot a guy."

"You were the only one who read the situation correctly. I wonder how many more people, including me, might've been sliced up by that guy."

Jill just shook her head, unwilling to look up.

Jess walked to us and knelt next to Jill. "We recovered three guns, dozens of stacks of currency, and several kilos of white powder from the next room."

"Did you look at that biker's prosthetic hand?" I asked.

Jess shook his head. "What about it?"

"His metal fingers were sharpened into claws. We couldn't see them inside his glove, so the deputies didn't know what was going on as he was shredding them. Jill's the only one who realized what was happening and reacted appropriately." I froze. "Where were you guys when I said, 'Mickey Mouse?'"

"We never heard anyone say Mickey Mouse until a deputy yelled it into his radio."

"I said it at least three times. The damned hooker was undressing me, and I finally popped the window and started yelling it outside."

"Where's your coat?"

"The hooker peeled it off me."

"Did it land on top of the mic?"

I rolled my eyes. "I don't know. Maybe."

"We'll check it after we clear the crime scene."

We heard the gurney clatter as the EMTs loaded the first deputy on it. The FBI agent was still holding a compress tight to his neck as they rolled past us.

"I hope he makes it," I said to no one in particular.

Rick, the sheriff, came out of the room and walked to us. He knelt next to Jill and me. "You're bloody, Fletcher. Do you need the EMTs?"

I shook my head. "This is all from your deputy."

"Well, thank God for that. I thought maybe that guy had taken a slice out of you, too."

The elevator opened and two more EMTs ran down the hallway to the open door.

Jill looked up. "How is the deputy with the sliced neck?"

The sheriff didn't answer immediately. "It'll be touch and go. The highway patrol is picking up his wife. They're taking him to Rapid City where there's a trauma surgeon scrubbing up and a surgical suite waiting. Beyond that, he's in God's hands."

The second gurney rattled past with the deputy whose arm was in a bandage as large as my thigh. One of the entry team deputies followed behind and stopped when he got to us. He put his back against the wall and slid down next to Jill.

He leaned his head back. "Jill."

"Yeah."

"I misread what was going on. Thanks for covering my butt."

Jill turned and frowned at him. "What?"

"I thought the biker was on drugs and was thrashing around…I don't know what I thought. But I didn't pull the trigger. I…" The deputy looked at the sheriff. "You ought to give Jill a medal, Rick. She pulled our butts out of the fire. If Charlie lives it's because she stopped the theatrics and let us get first aid before he bled out." He drew a deep breath. "Hell, all of us could've been in the back of an ambulance if she hadn't caught on to what was happening."

Jess got up and pulled the sheriff down the hall. They talked in muted tones, looking back at us.

Jill watched them for a while. "What's that all about?"

"I suspect that's an unofficial shooting review board."

"And…"

"And they're trying to figure out what to do with you."

"It's easy. I'll give them my gun and badge and we can go back to the ranch. I hope Chet and Daddy haven't finished off all that bourbon because I feel like getting a little drunk."

I pulled her up. "None of that is happening."

"Why not?"

"Because you're a damned hero again. They don't take badges away from heroes. They trot them out in front of reporters to give them ribbons and plaques."

Rick Wilson separated from Jess and walked to us. "Jill, I need your weapon. The state crime lab will have to compare the bullets that killed the biker to ones from your gun. Since you're the only person who fired a gun, it's a formality, but it's got to happen. I'll get it back to you tomorrow."

Jill took the gun out of her holster and handed it, butt first, to the sheriff. He ejected the magazine and the shell in the chamber. Then he shifted the gun to his left hand and extended his right hand. "Thank you both. I hardly know what to say beyond that."

He turned away, then stopped and turned back to us. "I was extremely skeptical about allowing you two into this operation, but Jess said you were two of the best law enforcement people he's ever worked with. I had a hard time accepting that, you being park rangers, but he's never steered me wrong. I let go of the reins on that decision. Jess was right. You two are as fine as they come."

A man in an FBI bullet proof vest came running down the hall and pulled Jess aside. They had an animated discussion that ended

220

with Jess pulling out his cellphone and walking to the far end of the hallway.

I nudged Jill. "Something else is up."

"Like what?"

"I don't know but it's got Jess worked up."

The phone call went on for several minutes. As soon as he disconnected, Jess punched in another number and started a second conversation. He waved the FBI agent down the hall as he wrapped up the conversation and the man ran past us. He didn't wait for the elevator and I heard him taking the steps two at a time.

Jess pulled his other agents out of the motel rooms and had a hushed conversation resulting in them rushing down the stairs. He looked at us, weighing something, then he knelt next to Jill. "The Custer County sheriff has been watching the cabin where we think the gang has been staying. It appears somebody got to them because they're packing and getting ready to bug out. I told the sheriff to intercept them, but he only has one car available to cover each of the possible exit routes, and whoever tries to stop them will be outgunned. I'm scrambling to get the highway patrol, the DEA, and my people up there, but we may not be able to respond in time."

Jess looked up as two Lawrence County deputies ran out of the motel room, responding to calls on their radios. "It'd be good to have a couple more cops there. Are you two up for some more action?"

Jill looked at me, then back at Jess. "The sheriff took my weapon to the crime lab."

"Can you shoot a shotgun?"

Jill pushed herself up. "When I turned eleven, Dad gave me one shell and told me I could have another if I hit the first sharptailed grouse I shot at."

"Did you ever get a second shell?" Jess asked.

"I shot my limit most times we went out."

Jess smiled. "I've got a Remington pump in back of the Suburban. Leave your truck here."

Jess put Jill in the front seat of his SUV, and I rode in the back. We sped to Custer on snow-covered roads at speeds I never would've attempted without four-wheel drive. Jess switched his radio to the police frequency, and we heard voices from multiple agencies reporting their locations and being directed to positions backing up Custer County deputies.

The dispatcher's voice came through. "Be advised the suspects are apparently monitoring this frequency. They've just left the driveway and have turned south in two pickups and a minivan. There appear to be five women in the minivan who may be hostages."

Jess shook his head. "I was afraid they might be keeping girls at the cabin and rotating them to the motels. This could be a real cluster..." he paused and looked at Jill. "A real mess."

Jill looked at him. "You know, I've worked around young rangers my entire career. I doubt you could use a phrase I haven't heard before."

Jess glanced at her. "Yeah, but it's unprofessional."

The radio announced the reinforcement of the southern roadblock by a DEA team, but the bikers hadn't appeared. The northern roadblock had been reinforced by the highway patrol and that team was moving south.

"We've got fresh tracks going up a driveway."

Jess shook his head. "More hostages are not what we need."

We arrived at the barricaded driveway twelve minutes later. The road was jammed with vehicles with flashing lights, and we could see a curl of smoke rising from a chimney on the hidden side of a far ridge. The Custer County sheriff ran to Jess. "I've got guys on foot trying to flank the house, but the terrain is open, and the snow is making it tough to make headway."

The words were hardly out of his mouth when we heard gunfire. The radio squawked, "We're taking fire from the house. I'm behind some round hay bales, but there's no way I can approach any closer."

A second voice came through. "I'm behind a ridgeline, but it's wide open from here to the house. Every time I poke my head up someone takes a pot shot at me."

Jess shook his head. "Is there a way to get close from a different direction?"

The sheriff shook his head. "There's a swampy lake a couple hundred yards behind the house, but the cattails won't provide much cover. Our best bet may be to have the power company shut off the electricity and we'll freeze them out."

Jess put his hands over his uncovered ears. "Who do you think will freeze first us, or them?"

"I see four people running toward the barn," the radio announced.

Jess shook his head. "What's in the barn they'd want? A tractor? Horses?"

The sheriff stared into the distance. "It's hard to say. There's a tractor or two and a baler. They might be modern ranchers and have four-wheel ATVs."

"Sounds like small engines," the radio announced.

The sheriff looked at Jess. "They're going to make a run for it."

Jess frowned. "Going where? We've got cops coming in from all over covering all the towns. South is just open country with nothing but the parks between here and the state line."

"Maybe they've got a hunting shack up in the high country. It could take days for us to find them and longer to get a team near them on snow machines."

"I've got four people on snowmobiles going west." The radio announced.

Jess jumped into the Suburban. "C'mon. We'll parallel their path and see if we can cut them off."

I got in the front seat and Jill jumped in the back. I could hear her scrambling into the storage space and unzipping a gun case. Then she pumped the shotgun to chamber a shell.

"There's a spare box of shells behind the seat, Jill."

We crested a hill with a pair of sheriff's department SUVs on our bumper. In the distance I could see the two snowmobiles racing parallel to us, cutting tracks across an ocean of white. The blizzard had created a featureless landscape interrupted only by a large oval of cattails.

"Uh oh," Jill said from the back.

"What?" I asked.

"The cattails. It hasn't been cold enough to freeze the lakes. The ice can't be…"

The lead snowmobile cut across the line of cattails and slowed. The driver revved the engine sending a spray of slush skyward.

Jill shook her head. "They're city kids. They don't know what they're doing."

The second machine veered left and got bogged down in fluffy snow held by the cattails. The driver revved the engine and bounded over a drift, but his impact smashed the ice. The snowmobile disappeared from view.

Jess hit the brakes causing chattering as the antilock mechanism engaged on the slippery road. We slowed, then slid to a stop. Jess grabbed the radio mic, but one of the sheriff's vehicles announced the lake situation before he could press the transmit button. I jumped out of the SUV and was ready to run to the snowmobiles across the ditch and two hundred yards of open field when I felt Jill's hand on my arm.

"Don't."

"But they'll drown."

Jess stood next to us in front of the Suburban and we were joined by the sheriff's deputies.

Jill pulled me close. We watched as the bikers tried to pull themselves onto the surrounding ice, only to have it collapse under their weight.

"Poor bastards," one of the deputies said, making no effort to move toward the flailing men.

I was baffled. "Why aren't we...?"

Jill shook her head. "They're dead. We couldn't get to them in ten minutes. They'll be hypothermic and slip under the water before we'd get halfway across the field of knee-deep snow."

A deputy requested assistance from the fire department. "We'll need a dive team to recover the bodies."

"I feel like we should do something," I said.

The deputy next to me summed up his feeling, "Fuck 'em. They're the scum of the earth and they're saving the taxpayers a lot of money."

* * *

Jess drove back to the farmhouse where we watched deputies load the five women into SUVs. I watched a blonde wearing a BHSU hoodie, climb into the second vehicle.

Jill nudged me. "There's the woman missing from the campground."

Jess drove us back to the motel and the National Park Service pickup. Jill wanted to drive back to the ranch, so I handed her the keys. "Why do you want to drive?"

"I don't have to think about the motel shooting and the drowning bikers if I'm concentrating on the road."

Jill handed me her phone. "Call the park."

I punched in the phone number for Wind Cave National Park and asked for the superintendent. "Chris, we found out how your backpacker died."

"Really? I mean, great! Tell me it wasn't a cougar."

"It wasn't a cougar. We caught a guy with a prosthetic hand. He'd sharpened the fingertips like razors and was using his prosthesis like a claw."

"No shit? How did you figure that out?"

"It's a long story that'll be on the evening news, but we caught him in a sting. I think we also have the missing woman. Last I saw there was a blonde wearing a BHSU hoodie being arrested by the Lawrence County sheriff.

They'll ID her through fingerprints, but I suspect she's going to explain the whole story about the dead backpacker."

"That's great. Thanks."

"It's not as great as it seems. The biker with the claw died during the arrest."

"You won't be able to close the case?"

"We'll close it. I'll have the pathologist compare the backpacker's wounds to the prosthetic hand. We might get the woman to explain what happened too."

"Say hi to Jill."

"Hang on." I switched my cellphone to speaker. "You're on speaker. Jill's sitting next to me."

"Hi, Jill. Thanks for coming north and helping with the investigation. It was nice to reconnect with you after all these years."

"Thanks, Chris. I hope we cross paths again some time. If you get down to Corpus Christi, you can look us up." Jill's voice was tight, and her comments clipped.

"Is everything all right? You sound like you're mad."

"It's not you. It's…"

I shut down the speaker. "We just had a tense standoff with the biker and his girlfriends, then we joined the FBI and Custer County in the apprehension of the rest of the bikers. Jill's very stressed out. She was part of the sting entry team…she had to fire her weapon to protect another officer."

Chris was silent for a moment. "I have a hard time relating to that. The biggest stress in my life is dealing with budget cuts, nothing compared to an armed standoff. You guys have a safe trip back to Texas."

"Thanks Chris. Enjoy the South Dakota winter."

"Yeah, like that's possible."

I shut down the phone.

"Thanks for not telling him I killed the biker. I'm not ready to talk about it."

Chapter Thirteen

Chet's pickup was out of the ditch, and it was dark when we got back to the ranch. Finding only Chet's snow encrusted pickup in the driveway and no other vehicles, Jill looked confused. "I guess everyone must've gone somewhere."

Molly wasn't at the stove, cooking, which made it feel emptier. Jill saw a note on the table and walked over to read it. I was taking my boots off when she yelled, "Put your boots back on. We're going to Rapid City."

I trotted to the pickup behind her. "What's going on?"

"Give me the keys!"

I threw the keys to her and got in the passenger side of the National Park Service vehicle. She flipped the switches for the lights and siren, then peeled out of the driveway spitting ice and gravel.

"What's going on?"

"Chet had a heart attack."

I pulled out my phone and realized I'd turned it off when I'd gone on the sting. There was no Wi-Fi, and I was down to one bar of service. My phone chimed repeatedly as messages loaded.

"Did you get any calls from them?"

I listened to message after message from Molly and Mom, first telling us Chet was having chest pain, then more saying an ambulance was on the way, the ambulance was there and Chet was having a heart attack, the ambulance was leaving for the hospital, then they were following the ambulance to the hospital. The last one was from Jess, telling me my mother had contacted the FBI duty officer and asked him to pass a message that they were at the Rapid City hospital.

Jill glanced at me repeatedly as she sped down the snow-covered roads. "What?"

"They've been trying to reach us for hours. The last message was relayed from the FBI office saying they were at the Rapid City hospital."

"Call your mother's cellphone."

I pulled up her number and listened to it ring. "I don't think they allow cellphones in the hospital."

I dialed Matt Mattson, my boss, and explained the day's events. Jill had been speeding down the side roads. She accelerated hard when we hit the interstate, passing cars who moved aside in response to our lights and siren.

Nearing the hospital, I dialed Jess Pond's cellphone. I explained what was going on and asked if he could get information about where we could find Chet and our family. He called me back in one minute and told me to go to the emergency room.

Jill left the lights flashing and parked with two wheels on the sidewalk in front of the emergency entrance. Molly, Al, and Mom were in the waiting room. Molly and Mom jumped up when we walked in.

"What's happening?" Jill asked.

"Chet started having chest pain when they pulled his stupid truck out of the ditch. He's bullheaded and had to shovel around it himself while your dad pulled with the tractor. The pain got worse when he came in, but he wouldn't go to the doctor. Ronnie called an ambulance when he couldn't stand the pain."

Mom looked frustrated. "He wanted us to drive him home so he could lay down."

Jill obviously understood. "So, what's happening?"

"No one is telling us anything. They'll only talk to Chet's family."

Jill marched up to the desk and spoke softly to the receptionist. The person at the desk picked up the phone and made a call.

I joined Jill and sidled up to her. "What's going on?"

"The doctor is coming out to speak with Chet's daughter. You're his son-in-law."

I looked at her and suppressed a smile.

A doctor came from behind double doors, obviously looking for someone. Jill walked to

232

him and put out her hand. "You're Dad's doctor?"

He smiled and directed us to a small room off the waiting area, closing the door behind us. "Your dad had a massive heart attack. They took him to surgery as soon as we got the cardiac surgeon's road open. He's still in surgery."

"What's his prognosis?"

"There was a long time between the onset of symptoms and the surgeon's arrival, so we can't express much optimism."

Jill teared up, and I pulled her close. "Thanks, doctor. Please keep us updated."

Mom, Molly, and Al were waiting impatiently for us and read Jills tears as the worst news. Molly engulfed us in a hug. "He's gone?"

Jill dug a tissue out of her pocket. "He's in surgery but the doctor said there was a long delay between his symptoms starting and getting him into surgery."

Molly spun around and poked Al in the chest. "Damn your bullheadedness."

"What did I do?"

Molly gave him a withering glare. "You two are so bullheaded you won't admit when you're sick or need help. One of these days it's going to kill you."

Mom hugged Jill. "They've got him in surgery. They can do wonders."

An hour later, the receptionist called for Jill and we walked to her desk, expecting the worst.

233

"Your father is in the recovery room. They'll move him to the ICU as soon as he comes around."

* * *

We sat in the ICU waiting room with two other families, all of us with red-rimmed eyes. Boxes of tissues sat on every flat surface, a coffee maker rested on a corner table, and a phone sat on an end table in the opposite corner. A woman had been on the phone continuously since we arrived, dialing one family member after another, tearfully telling them to come down as soon as possible.

At 2 a.m. a doctor in scrubs walked in and everyone looked up. "Is Chet's family here?"

Jill got up and the doctor waved us to the corner by the coffee maker. "He's out of surgery and in a room. He had four blocked coronary arteries. The blockages were too large for stents, so I stripped veins from his legs and did a bypass. I wish I could be optimistic, but areas of his heart had been without blood flow for a long time. We'll know a lot more in a couple of days. We're just getting him set up in a room. A nurse will let you know when you can go in to see him. No more than two visitors at a time, and please limit your visits to a few minutes. He's heavily sedated and may not be aware of you. The one thing we hear from patients after they recover is that they heard people talking to them even when they couldn't respond, so please be upbeat and let him know that you're there, and that you care."

It was nearly an hour later when the nurse came for Chet's family. Jill and Molly went in first. They were back in five minutes, both in tears. Jill sat next to me. "He's gray, on a respirator, and there's dozen tubes running into him. He didn't open his eyes, but we talked to him." Jill leaned her head on my shoulder. "They're going to wean him off the respirator in the morning. If he doesn't breathe on his own..."

A doctor came in and asked for Charlie Whitcomb's family. They huddled near the coffee maker and a young woman gasped when the doctor spoke. She was in tears and the family gathered around her.

Rick Wilson, the Lawrence County Sheriff walked in and was surprised to see Jill and me. "You guys came down to be with Charlie's family?"

"No, Jill's godfather is in the ICU. He had a heart attack shoveling this afternoon."

Rick motioned for Jill and me to follow him. "Carrie, this is Jill and Doug Fletcher. They were in the room when Charlie was attacked. Doug did first aid and probably saved Charlie's life. Jill is the one who shot the attacker."

We shook hands with Carrie and her parents. "Thank you," she sobbed.

"How's he doing?" I asked.

"He lost a lot of blood and is unconscious, but stable."

Rick knelt next to Carrie. "I'm here, and there'll be a deputy at his side through this. Whatever you need, you just tell me, or the deputy and we'll make it happen. Okay?" Rick pulled a badge out of his shirt pocket and put it in Carrie's hand. "Take care of this. Charlie will need it when he gets back on duty."

Carrie clutched the badge and nodded.

I met the sheriff at the door. "Do we know how bad Charlie is?"

Rick nodded to the hallway. "You slowed the blood loss, but he was pumping arterial blood until the EMTs got him to the ER. They gave him blood downstairs and during surgery. Let's hope it was enough and in time."

A haggard man wearing a sport coat over jeans and a plaid shirt walked toward us. His graying hair stood on end, and he had a leather portfolio under one arm. He made a beeline for the sheriff.

"What the hell wouldn't wait until morning, Rick?"

"I've got a deputy in the ICU and another who was stitched up in the emergency room and sent home. Both were part of a prostitution and drug sting we ran this afternoon that turned sour."

"So, what the hell makes it so important you dragged me out of bed at this ungodly hour?"

"Mac, I wanted you here in case Charlie Whitcomb comes around and can make a statement."

"If he comes around?"

"He lost a lot of blood and he's been unconscious."

The unkempt man scratched his armpit. "What do you expect him to tell me that's so important?"

I tried to slip away but the sheriff grabbed my arm. "Mac McQuiston, this is Doug Fletcher, from the National Park Service. Mac's the county attorney."

We shook hands.

"Mac, Doug was the bait in our sting. There was a biker in the adjoining room, and he walked in before my entry team breached the door. Doug fought him off until Charlie tried to cuff the biker. Then Charlie got his neck slashed and Hank Parker tried to grab the biker and got his arm slashed down to the tendons."

"Sounds like your guys fucked up."

I was too tired to be polite. "The biker had a prosthetic hand he'd sharpened like a cat's claw. It was inside a glove and we didn't know he was going to do anything more than scratch people until he ripped Charlie's throat open with it."

The attorney looked skeptical, so the sheriff pulled out pictures of the prosthesis.

"We believe he also slashed the neck of a Wind Cave National Park visitor last week and left him to bleed out. He's been using the dead man's ATM and charge cards, and the FBI has been monitoring him. When they searched the guy's motel room, they recovered three guns, stacks of cash, and two kilos of drugs."

"Great. So, what of that wouldn't wait until tomorrow morning? I need that for the arraignment, but not at…" the attorney looked at his watch, "three a.m."

"There won't be an arraignment. The biker's dead."

"Dead? Someone shot him?"

"Mac, his hand was a deadly weapon. He slashed two deputies and was going for more. Charlie might not live through the night, and Hank Parker will probably need several surgeries to repair the muscles and ligaments in his arm. We're lucky Doug's partner saw what was going on and shot the guy before he tore up more people."

"Geez, Rick. The guy was unarmed. You couldn't restrain and arrest him?"

Rick held out the pictures of the prosthetic hand. "He was wearing a glove over this…killing device. We thought he was trying to scratch people. He was trying to claw them. Charlie might die from his wound."

McQuiston looked at the pictures, then the sheriff pulled out photos of the wounds on Hank Parker's arm and Charlie's neck.

The sheriff pulled out another picture of the blood-soaked motel room.

"This blood is all from Charlie and Hank?"

"Yes! That's what I'm trying to tell you. It was a bloodbath, and this biker was swinging his hand around attempting to claw my guys who were trying to cuff him."

"Okay. He was a grave threat to the arrest team. Why didn't they just back off?"

"Mac, we had six people in a little motel room. Doug got knocked down. I've got one guy with his neck slashed and bleeding out on the floor, another with his forearm slashed. There's a naked hooker screaming and this biker swinging his claw around. There was no backing off."

"Okay. I've got the picture. It's chaos. You've got people down. Who shot and how many people did he hit?"

"My wife, Jill Fletcher, a National Park Service law enforcement ranger wearing an FBI bullet proof vest, shot. The only person she hit was the biker."

"How many shots did she take?"

The sheriff put up his hand to silence me. "She shot until the threat was neutralized. Five shots were fired. All five struck the biker in the chest."

"She didn't miss? She didn't hit anyone else? No stray shots went through the walls endangering people in adjoining rooms?"

"She took five shots. Three shots, then she reassessed the threat and fired two more."

McQuiston looked at me. "Your wife did that?"

"Yes, sir."

McQuiston looked at the sheriff. "So, what do you want me to do?"

"I talked to Jess Pond, the FBI Special Agent in Charge of the Rapid City office. We're in agreement that the shooting was justified and if Jill Fletcher hadn't fired on the biker, more people would've been injured or killed. We believe her quick action probably saved at least one life."

"Sounds like a justified shooting. Maybe you should hire her to train your deputies to shoot."

The sheriff nodded. "I just wanted to make sure you understood what happened before the news gets hold of this and some liberal editor tries to make it look like an unarmed biker was shot. You're good with this. I can release Jill Fletcher's weapon and no charges will be filed."

McQuiston thought for a moment. "Theoretically, I'm in agreement. I'd like to talk to this Fletcher woman before I sign off."

I walked into the waiting room and signaled for Jill to join us.

"Mac, this is Jill Fletcher. Mac is the county attorney. He'd like to talk to you about this afternoon."

Jill stiffened. "I'm a little stressed out right now. My godfather is in the ICU, and we've been up for twenty hours."

Mac nodded. "I understand, but could you briefly tell me what happened before you fired your weapon?"

Jill closed her eyes for a second, then retold the story of the entry, the slashing biker, the screaming hooker, me helpless on the floor and pulling down on the biker as he was reaching out to slash another deputy.

The attorney opened his notebook. "How many shots did you fire?"

"I shot three times, then I saw that the biker was still a threat and was still reaching out to slash at my team member, so I fired twice more. At that point, he'd clutched his chest with the claw and wasn't a threat anymore, so I held my gun on him and he fell to the floor. I kept my gun on him while people started first aid on the injured deputies."

"Did you fire at him while he was on the floor?"

"No sir. He was standing and presenting a threat when I fired."

McQuiston closed his notebook and looked at me. "And that's what you saw?"

"I was unarmed for the sting. I'd fought off the guy with a lamp, then fell to the floor when he was slashing at the deputies. If Jill hadn't fired, I expect he would've come after me next."

McQuiston shook Jill's hand. "I've got no problem with this. I won't charge you. If anything, Rick should give you a medal."

Jill looked toward the ICU where a nurse was motioning for her to come. "Excuse me, but my godfather is not doing well, and the nurse wants me."

McQuiston tucked his portfolio back under his arm. "Fletcher, it seems like your wife is quite a cop. Sounds like you're lucky to be alive, too."

The sheriff steered the attorney into the waiting room where he introduced Charlie's wife and family. They walked to Charlie's ICU room.

Jill came back with tears in her eyes.

"What's happening?" I asked.

"Chet opened his eyes and recognized me. He squeezed my hand. They've got a respiratory therapist coming and they hope to wean him off the respirator and down to an oxygen cannula."

I thought about McQuiston's questions and the sheriff's comment about the media getting the story. "Come outside with me."

"What?"

"There are signs all over prohibiting cellphone use. Let's go outside and call Matt."

"Oh crap. If this story gets to the wire services before Matt calls his bosses…"

"Yes!" I said as we trotted to the front entrance.

I pulled up my boss's cellphone number, punched it in, and handed the phone to Jill. I left her to talk with Matt while I moved the pickup off the sidewalk and into a parking spot. When I got back, Jill was nodding and giving brief answers to questions.

She handed me the phone. "Hi, Matt."

"What's with you two? Can't you just go home for Christmas and open presents like normal people?"

"We came here to investigate a suspicious death. Christmas was incidental."

"Right. Well, I need to make some phone calls and let the chain of command know what happened. When you get to a computer, you both have to fill out incident reports."

"Jill's folks don't own a computer."

"Then buy a laptop and go to a library with Wi-Fi. The reports have to be in within twenty-four hours." Matt paused. "Mandy just called Jill's cellphone and it rolled over to voicemail."

"Yeah, her battery died."

"I'll have Mandy call your number as soon as we hang up."

I handed Jill the phone. "Mandy's going to call you."

Chapter Fourteen

We went back to the ranch to get some rest after Chet got weaned off the respirator. The phone buzzed at seven, after I'd had about two hours of sleep.

"Yeah."

"Fletcher?"

I was trying to shake the cobwebs from my mind. "Yes, what's up?"

"There's going to be a news conference at the Lawrence County courthouse at eleven a.m. We'd like you and Jill to be there."

I groaned. "Who is this? Is this an offer or an order?"

"This is Rick Wilson and I'd like to introduce you and Jill as part of the team at our sting operation."

"If it's all the same to you, I'd rather get some sleep."

"I'd really like you to be here. We've got Rapid City and Sioux Falls television stations coming as well as half a dozen newspapers."

"Rick, I'm not photogenic and Jill is shy. Just go ahead without us if we don't show up."

Jill overheard the conversation and rolled over. "You know, we're not going to be able to get out of this."

"Go back to sleep. We didn't even bring uniforms this trip."

I was almost asleep when the phone buzzed again. "Fletcher."

"Hey, Doug, it's Matt. I just got a call from the National Park Service's Midwest Regional Director. There's going to be a news conference in Lead at eleven. The National Park Service wants you and Jill there, in uniform."

"We haven't had any sleep. We don't have uniforms along. I don't know where Lead is. And I'm pissed off because people keep calling and waking me up."

"Listen to me carefully. As a friend, I'm asking you to go to the news conference."

"As a friend, I'm telling you I have only had two hours of sleep and I'm not going to a news conference."

"Give the phone to Jill."

I handed Jill the phone and laid down. I heard her say, "Yes, Matt," repeatedly.

She lay down and put the phone on the nightstand. "We're going to the news conference."

"Have a good time."

"You missed the operative word, 'we.' We are going to the news conference."

I pulled the quilt over my head. "You're the hero. You don't need me."

"Matt explained it clearly. He ordered me to attend the conference. Because you are technically his equivalent rank, he can only request you to attend. However, if you refuse his request, you'll be getting a call from his boss who *will* order you to be there."

"It's a damned dog and pony show for the sheriff."

Jill pulled the quilt back. "Take a shower and shave. I'll find something presentable for us to wear."

* * *

There were already three news vans on site with dish antennae up when we met Rick Wilson in his office at ten thirty. He stood and shook our hands. "Looks like you got a call from the National Park Service. I had hoped you'd show up in your Smokey Bear hats."

"Smokey stayed in Texas," Jill explained. "Doug borrowed Daddy's best Stetson."

I frowned, having lost the argument that my purple Minnesota Vikings stocking cap would be adequate.

Jess Pond walked in wearing a western outfit including jeans and boots. His one dressy accessory was a bolo tie.

Rick nodded to Jess, then turned to us. "Pin your National Park Service badges to your jackets and pull back your coats so your holsters show. You're going to look like the western version of National Park Service cops. Okay?"

The press conference took place in the courthouse lobby. I stood behind Jill who'd been directed to stand next to the sheriff. Rick was generous with his praise and thanked the FBI, the National Park Service, and singled out Jill Fletcher as the person who stepped forward when most needed and had saved several lives. The official news conference ended, and Jill was cut away from the other officers and singled out for one-on-one interviews. She smiled, acted professional, repeatedly crediting the team, and minimizing her role. I took off my badge and tried to look like a local who was hanging around the fringe of the crowd.

A reporter I recognized from the Gillette, Wyoming newspaper was struggling to get anyone to speak with him. He spied me drinking coffee in a corner and hustled to my side. "Ranger Fletcher, tell me what happened at the motel."

I tried to wave him off, saying the sheriff had covered all the key points. He was undeterred and stayed after me.

I looked him in the eye. "This is what really happened, and you're getting an exclusive." He lit up like I'd just made his day, week, and year. I spent ten minutes filling him in on the planning, the hooker's use of a dating website, the exchange of text pictures, the failed Mickey Mouse code word, the biker flying into the room, and the deputies getting clawed before Jill took the biker down.

The young reporter looked at his notes. "None of this was covered by the sheriff."

"You go ask my wife or any of the deputies who were on scene, and you'll get the same story, and you're the only one who'll have the gory details."

Jill finally broke away from the crowd and found me. "Let's get out of here."

We were walking out the courthouse door when Rick Wilson yelled my name. He walked to us and nodded to an alcove in the lobby. "We've got seven women in the jail, and they've lawyered up, so we haven't been able to talk to them. The county attorney had a call from the Assistant U.S. Attorney for South Dakota. Because of the interstate drug and prostitution charges, they've been in touch with Jess Pond and they are willing to deal if the women will testify against the gang. It's a little touchy, because a couple of the women called Denver and the attorney who showed up represents the gang and he's telling them they'll be taken care of if they don't make a deal. I assume he's also telling them they're dead if they *do* make a deal."

"Where's Jess?"

"He's down in the jail talking to the womens' attorney. He asked me to bring you over."

We followed Rick through the courthouse and into the jail. We had to check our cellphones and guns in lockers before being buzzed into the secure area.

Jill slid close to me as the doors banged shut behind us. "This makes me more claustrophobic than the cave."

Rick led us to the room with Jess and the lawyer, but I stopped him. "I'd like to talk to the blonde who was in the other motel room. The one wearing the hoodie."

"You can't question her. She's already spoken with her attorney and he's advised her not to answer any questions."

"Is she alone in a cell?"

"All we have is single cells."

"Take Jill and me to her cell. I'd like you to stay with us, too."

Rick gave me a questioning look but led us deeper into the jail. A female jailer unlocked a cell and the three of us walked in. The blonde looked very young without her makeup. She was wearing jailhouse orange coveralls and flipflops. She was lying on a bunk with a thin mattress. A stainless-steel toilet and wash basin were in the back corner. Aside from that, the cell was barren.

Rick nodded to the woman. "We ran her prints. This is Patricia Carson of Colorado Springs. She's been arrested three times for soliciting prostitution and twice for drug possession. She's pled out to misdemeanors and has never been in prison."

I knelt down to her eye level. "I know you have a lawyer, and you don't have to answer any questions, but I'd like to tell you a couple things."

Her eyes were hard, like she'd seen too much in her young life. "Not without my lawyer."

"Your lawyer works for the Scorpions. He's interested in protecting them, not you. The sheriff recovered several kilos of drugs, guns, and thousands of dollars. We've spoken with the U.S. Attorney and you're going to be charged with interstate drug dealing, prostitution, and RICO violations."

"What's a RICO violation?"

"It's a federal law used to charge people who are acting in support of organized crime. The minimum RICO sentence is fifteen years in a federal prison. If you're also convicted of the drug and interstate prostitution charges, you won't get out of jail until you're sixty."

"Tell it to my lawyer."

"Your lawyer doesn't want you to plea bargain because you'd be turning against his clients, the Scorpions. They're willing to let you spend the next thirty years in prison to protect their operations."

"So, what are you offering?"

"I can get a public defender in here and the U.S. Attorney will plea bargain your sentence down to a few months."

"I'd never live long enough to testify. I'll take my chances with my attorney."

Jill cleared her throat. "We could talk to the Feds about witness protection and relocation."

The blonde looked at Jill like she was seeing her for the first time. "Who are you?"

"I'm a federal law enforcement officer. I'll personally speak with the U.S. Attorney about witness protection." Jill paused. "Have you ever seen a woman who's spent thirty years in prison? Even the women who spend that much time in a minimum-security facility come out shells of their former selves. They're broken and tired. They've got no friends or family. They move into a section-eight high rise and live off welfare and food shelf pickings until they die."

Patricia threw her legs over the side of the bed and sat up. "The life I've been living isn't any bed of roses. A federal lockup might be better than turning tricks and getting beaten up."

If Jill was shocked, she didn't show it. "You're right. Making a living on your back isn't much of a life, especially when you're turning all the money over to some leech who beats you up if you look at him crosswise."

The blonde glanced at Jill's wedding ring. "What would you know about my life. You've got a husband, a couple kids, a three-bedroom house with two bathrooms. You've probably got a minivan with the white stick figures of your family and pets in the back window. Don't look down your nose at me. You have no idea who I am or what I've been through."

Jill shook her head. "Any woman who makes a couple bad decisions and hooks up with the wrong guy could be right where you're sitting. I got lucky and landed with a good guy who respects me and treats me well. He's never hit me, threatened me, or even sworn at me, but

I passed up on a few others along the way to here." Jill paused. "I'm offering you a reset button on your life. Talk to the U.S. Attorney and see what he's got to offer, then decide if that doesn't sound better than rotting away in a women's prison for the next thirty years."

"My attorney won't let me."

"You get to choose your attorney. All you have to do is ask for a public defender and you'll never see the gang's attorney again."

"What about Brenda?"

"Brenda was the woman in the other motel room?"

Patricia and Rick both nodded.

"This offer is exclusive to you. If you take it first, you're in. If Brenda, or one of the other five women from the cabin take it, they're in and our offer to you is rescinded."

"You found the others at the cabin?"

"Yes."

Patricia nodded, like that was good. "And the guys?"

"They're dead."

Patricia shuddered. "Can I think about it?"

I stood up. "We're going to Brenda's cell now and if she says yes, you may be out of luck."

Patricia looked at the floor. "I'm fucked any way I go." She let out a breath. "Okay. My attorney is fired. Get me a decent public defender and send in the U.S. Attorney. But keep me away from the other prisoners. I want to live through this."

Jill stepped up to Patricia and put out her hand. "Where I grew up, a handshake was as good as a signed contract."

Patricia looked at Jill's hand, then shook it. "I hope you're for real, Mrs. Federal Cop."

We walked out of the cell, but Jill stopped at the door and turned. "How'd you get Parker's PIN number?"

"He had it all on his cellphone with his social security number, his bank accounts, and his computer passwords. I'm sure the Scorpions have a hundred charge cards in his name with a million bucks in charges and cash advances by now. I can't believe anyone is that stupid."

"Some people are very trusting."

Patricia rolled her eyes. "We call them sheep. They're just waiting to be fleeced."

Chapter Fifteen

The jailer closed the interview room door. I was ready to leave but the sheriff nodded toward a different interview room. "We pulled out a girl who wants to talk to the park rangers."

"Why isn't she in a cell like the others?"

Rick took a deep breath. "She's underage. We're waiting for family protective services to talk to her, then she'll be charged as a minor."

Jill looked like she'd been through hell. Her eyes darted from the jailer to the interview room. "Who else has she spoken to?"

"She says she'll only talk to the rangers."

I let out a breath and nodded. "Let's talk to her."

The girl was resting her head on her arms. Her head snapped up when the door opened. I followed Jill into the interview room, and we stood by the table. The girl eyed us suspiciously.

"I want to talk to park rangers."

The girl was slender and looked like she was no more than fourteen with skin-tight jeans, and her hair in a ponytail. She was wearing a dirty hoodie with black sleeves. It had a BHSU logo printed across her chest. Her eyes said she'd seen much more than any average teen.

I pulled the badge off my belt and held it up. "I'm a National Park Service investigator. My partner is a law enforcement ranger."

Jill pulled back a metal chair and sat across from the girl. "What's your name?" she asked softly.

"Angie."

"What was your name when you went to BHSU?"

The girl looked down at the logo on her hoodie then back at Jill. "I wasn't a student. I bought the sweatshirt at a garage sale."

"You've been through a lot."

The girl's eyes narrowed. "So?"

I sat down. "Why did you want to talk to us?"

"What happened at the park, that was a federal crime, right?"

I clipped my badge back to my belt. "I'm not sure what crime you're talking about."

Angie gave me a withering glare. "Don't bullshit me, okay. I know you've been all over Keystone and Custer looking for me and the only reason park rangers would be asking about me is because of what happened at Wind Cave."

"What happened to the camper?"

"I had nothing to do with it. Steve was stupid and sweet. And…I had nothing to do with what Zag did."

"Who's Zag?" Jill asked.

"Zig Zag. The guy with the claw."

"Do you know his name?"

Angie shook her head. "They all have nicknames. That's all I ever heard him called."

"Have you been arrested before?"

Angie looked at the corner. "That's how the Scorpions got me. I was busted for meth. I was broke and my supplier said he could get me the best lawyer if I'd cooperate after I got off."

"Your cooperation was costly," Jill said, as a statement, not a question.

Angie nodded, but didn't reply. I assume her 'cooperation' cost her whatever life she'd had before the arrest.

Jill leaned forward. "Tell us what happened with Steve Palmer."

Angie hesitated, staring into the corner of the room. "It was just stupid. I mean, Palmer got in way over his head. I was working a bar in Custer. Zag was selling and I was delivering. Palmer was sitting at the bar and he hit on me. We did the usual verbal dating dance and I offered to party with him and told him it'd cost him. He didn't believe I was hooking, but then asked if I'd spend the weekend camping with him. I told him I had to use the bathroom and was going to walk out the back door, but Zag told me to go back and see how much I could get out of him for the weekend."

"Then what happened?" Jill asked.

"Zag told me to go with him and call for a pickup once I'd gotten cash out of the guy.

Steve didn't have much cash, so we went to an ATM, then we went to the campground. I mean, it's in the middle of nowhere out there. We did the usual stuff, you know… I hung around until morning. When Steve went to the bathroom, I used his phone to call Zag who got really mad. We'd driven to the park in the dark and I didn't know exactly where we were. Then Steve came back and started asking what a nice girl like me was doing in the business. He offered to take me to Mitchell and help me get clean and free."

"And then Zag showed up?"

"No, I was hanging around with Steve, you know, playing nice, like I was going to go with him and start over, but I knew the gang would track me down and drag me back. So, every time Steve was gone, I'd be on the phone trying to explain to Zag where I was."

"Eventually Zag found you. Then what happened?"

"Zag told Steve that he owed for all my lost working time and Steve tried to bargain with him." Angie looked away. "They were in the pickup, so I didn't hear everything that was going on, but Steve offered to buy me."

Jill frowned. "Buy you?"

Angie shrugged. "You know, come up with enough cash so Zag would let him take me away."

"How did Steve end up dead in the prairie?"

"He and Zag…I don't know. He must've told Steve they had to get away from the campground for the transaction." Angie looked away from us. "Zag gave me the keys to Steve's truck and told me to leave. That's the last I knew until Zag showed up in Rapid City."

"You weren't present when Zag killed Steve?" Jill asked.

Angie shook her head, not meeting Jill's eyes. "I thought maybe Zag had beaten him up or something, then he started using Steve's phone and charge cards and I was sure something worse had happened."

"You didn't ask?"

"You don't ask a pimp what happens to a John after you leave. You just move on." Angie paused. "What happens to me now? I mean, I didn't do anything to Steve."

"You're an accessory to his murder, you engaged in prostitution in a national park, and you stole his pickup from the park. The U.S. Attorney will try you for what happened in the park, and the county will press drug and prostitution charges for what was going on at the cabin."

Angie cried, but Jill restrained herself from consoling her. The crying stopped and Angie wiped her eyes with her sleeve, then looked at us. "What?"

"All done with the crocodile tears?" Jill asked.

Angie leaned back in the chair and glared at us.

"How old are you, Angie?"

"In people years or whore years?"

"What's your real name?" When Angie didn't answer, Jill added, "you know we'll get it from your fingerprints."

Angie looked at the corner of the room. "Jane Proctor."

Jill smiled. "Okay. How old is Jane Proctor and where did she live?"

"I was born in Omaha and I'm seventeen."

"How long have you been 'in the business?'"

"Three years."

Jill did the math and glanced at me. "Do you want to get clean and get out of the business, or should we just leave you alone and let you go to prison with the others?"

"What chance do I have at a normal life? I can't go back to Omaha. I doubt my mother is even alive. She's the one who got me arrested for selling to support her meth habit."

"Where's your father?"

Jane gave a brittle laugh. "I had a bunch of 'uncles' who'd stay around a few weeks or a few months, but I doubt my mother even knew who my biological father was. He was just some John who impregnated her when she was too high to be concerned about a condom."

Jill glanced at me and I shook my head. "We can talk to the U.S. Attorney and he might be willing to get you into a drug program and a juvenile facility where you can get a high school diploma and a chance at a 'real' life. In return, he'd want you to testify against the Scorpions."

Angie/Jane tensed. "They'd kill me."

"Three of them are already dead, including Zag, and there are other women who are going to bring down the rest of them. I think the DEA is probably raiding their houses and offices in Denver and Cheyenne right now. The Scorpions are gone, history. You can help nail the lid on the coffin."

"I'll talk to him, but I want details. I have to get out of the Midwest or the ones who plea bargain or escape will be hunting me…us down."

Jill pushed back her chair and I followed her out of the door. When Rick closed the door, I pulled Jill aside. "You didn't shake hands with her."

"She was…evasive. What'd you think?"

"I looked in her eyes and there's nothing there. Her soul is gone, probably ripped out of her by drugs and the Scorpions. She'll never leave the business. Even if she gets relocated, she'll look for a pimp or be working in a massage parlor in a month."

Rick nodded.

Jill put her hand on my arm. "You didn't believe her?"

"Hardly a word of what she said was the truth."

"How do you know?"

"Every time you asked her a direct question, she'd hesitate a fraction of a second while she looked into the corner."

"Like poker players, she had a 'tell?'"

"Exactly. I'll bet she was there when Palmer was murdered and all the backstory she fed us is pure fantasy."

"What do you think, sheriff?"

Rick shook his head. "She's been in the system and knows all the right words."

Jill closed her eyes. "So, what happens to her?"

I knew Jill was touched by the girl's story, but I'd heard too many tales of woe to be taken in by another drug-addict prostitute. "We'll talk to Jess and she'll be charged with a class B federal felony for her role in the murder. She'll be old and gray when she sees the outside world again."

"But she's so young. There are juvenile treatment options."

I steered Jill away from the interview room as the sheriff took Angie, or Jane, or whoever she really was, out of the interview room and into the jail. "I'll bet you a hundred bucks she's not a day under twenty-one."

Jill looked at me. "But…"

"It was her eyes. She's trying hard to look young so she commands top dollar as a teenaged hooker, but her eyes have that hardness, the vacant stare. She's been a working girl a long time. I imagine when her identification comes back, she'll have a string of prostitution arrests. It'd be interesting to compare her booking pictures over the years."

I put my hand on Jill's shoulder and steered her toward the exit. "Pretty soon you'll be as cynical as me."

We waited for the jailer to let us out of the holding area without speaking.

"I guess I understand why you're sometimes so skeptical of people's motives."

Jess met us in the lobby. "Are you guys ready to go back to the ranch?"

"My uncle is in the Rapid City hospital. Can you drive us back to the pickup?"

I filled in Jess about my suspicions about Angie.

He walked us to his SUV. "We'll get her history and have one of our best interrogators take a crack at her. If we had any hard evidence she'd set Palmer up, the U.S. Attorney might've gone for the death penalty."

I got in the front seat next to Jess. "Replay our interview with her. She admitted calling the killer to the park and stealing Palmer's pickup. That makes her an accessory to murder."

That comment stunned Jill, who sat in silence the rest of the ride to Rapid City.

* * *

We shook hands with Jess, then drove to the hospital in the park service pickup. I'd hoped Jill would talk about the shooting, the drownings, and the prostitutes, but she was deep in thought.

She finally looked at me. "Patricia repeated your line about most people being sheep."

The comment caught me off guard. "It's true."

"How can…" Jill shook her head.

"How can what?"

"How can you raise a kid so they're not just prey for some…animal?"

"You teach them right from wrong. You watch who they hang out with. You try to make them understand there are predators out there without making them paranoid. Then you hope for the best."

"That doesn't seem like enough. I mean, look at Angie/Jane. She's young and attractive, yet hard as steel. And Patricia, how did she end up where she is?"

"We don't know Patricia's backstory. She may have come from an abusive home or got in with the wrong crowd at school and started using drugs. She said you don't know her and even if we spent the time to talk to her, what we'd hear would be filtered. My experience with drugged up hookers is they'll tell you what they think you want to hear, and you can never drill down to their real story."

"This cop stuff sucks."

I patted Jill's knee. "That's the one thing about the National Park Service, we usually don't see the very worst of it. All we have to do is watch our herd of campers, who are mostly sheep, and try to keep the wolves at bay."

Molly was alone, watching the television in the ICU waiting room. She looked up when we walked in. "You two looked good on TV."

Jill ignored the compliment. "How's Uncle Chet?"

"He's breathing on his own. Why don't you go over and check on him?"

Jill left and I sat next to Molly. "How are you holding up?"

She leaned her head against my shoulder. "I'm dead tired. How about you?"

"I'm about the same." I looked around and realized we were alone and got a sinking feeling. "Where's the family of the deputy who was clawed?"

"He died about ten this morning."

I felt deflated. I thought back to holding a compress against his neck to stanch the bleeding and seeing the EMTs running the gurney to the elevator.

"The doctor came in and spoke with his wife. They're donating his organs. I heard something about heart, kidney, and liver transplant patients. He'll live on through them."

"If not for Jill's shooting skill, I might've been a transplant donor too."

"Jill's a hero?"

"Absolutely."

"Tell Al. Give him all the details you've never said to anyone."

"I'm not sure Jill will appreciate that."

"Doug, it's time for Al to understand that Jill is everything he'd ever hoped for in his children. Jill was the girl, always second best. Help him to understand that she's everything he'd ever hoped Junior would be…and maybe more."

"You don't think he knows that?"

"Chet knows that. He's been telling us that Jill's a gem for years. It's time Al hears that from someone else. Maybe he can let go of some of his grief and take pride in her."

Jill came back looking pleased. "Chet was awake and talking. He's weak and tired, but he said they're going to transfer him down to a surgical floor this afternoon. They're going to start him on some cardio therapy next week and probably get him into a rehab facility for a couple weeks."

Molly nodded. "We're going to put a hospital bed in Junior's room until he's well enough to go home."

I looked between Jill and Molly. "Do you think he'll ever be able to go back to living alone?"

Molly smiled. "He's at our house twelve hours a day already. This will just save him the drive back and forth." Molly paused. "You know I've had two men in my life for forty years. I'm married to Al, but Chet is like my brother."

* * *

Mom was drinking coffee and reading the newspaper at the kitchen table. She looked up when we came in and smiled. "The daughter-in-law who saved my son's life."

Jill shook her head but smiled. She got down two mugs and poured coffee for us. I took mine into the living room where Al was watching a game show on television.

"Did you see the news conference, Al?"

"Sheriff Wilson did a nice job of sharing the credit. He even had Jill alongside him."

"Did you read the article in the Gillette newspaper?"

"I don't know who their reporter spoke with, but he had a pretty wild story about the guy with the claw and Jill sounding like Annie Oakley."

"He talked to me. And I told him exactly what happened. If not for Jill, several people would've been badly hurt or killed, including me. I was trapped on the floor against the back wall without a way to protect myself. Jill saved my life."

Al made a dismissive gesture.

I took the remote off the table and turned off the television. "Jill is one of the best cops I've ever worked with. She's cool under pressure and she can outshoot 99% of the cops around. You raised one hell of a woman. She's incredible and I'm honored to be married to her."

Al stared at me, processing what I'd said. He reached for the remote, but I pulled it away. Jill and Mom stopped talking in the kitchen and listened to us.

"Al, Jill is everything you'd hoped any of your children would be. She led the horses out to rescue Chet. She stepped forward twice to fearlessly shoot men who were threatening the lives of others. She's caring and gentle, yet strong." I paused to let my words sink in.

Al stared at me and said, "Yes." His voice was raspy and filled with emotion.

"Have you told her you were proud of her?"

He nodded. "I told her that in Texas."

I shook my head. "Is that the only time you've said it?"

Al looked at me, then stared at the floor. Jill took a step toward us, but I put up my hand to stop her.

"She's standing right behind you, Al."

Al took a deep breath and got up from his recliner. He took a step toward Jill and hesitated.

"Daddy, I know you care…"

"What you've done this week, well, it's opened my eyes…again."

He paused and I thought he was done. Mom surprised me when she got up from the table and wrapped Jill in a hug. "You're amazing. I'm so lucky to have you for my daughter-in-law."

Al watched silently until Mom released her hug, then he took Jill's hand and rubbed her wedding ring with his thumb. "Somebody said there's no fool like an old fool. Chet's been telling me for thirty years what a wonderful person you are, and I thought he had stars in his eyes. Turns out, I was too busy looking over my shoulder to see what was in front of me. Chet and Doug are right. My little girl grew up into a smart, strong woman while I wasn't paying attention."

Jill hugged him. "Thanks, Daddy."

Al whispered something into her ear and tears ran down her face as Al patted her back. He stood back and nodded, to accentuate whatever he'd whispered to her. Then he walked to the bedroom and closed the door. I heard him sobbing.

Mom, Jill, and I hugged.

Mom pulled away. "I've got to call the airport to see if they've rebooked my flight."

I followed Jill into the bedroom and closed the door. "Are you okay?"

She shook her head and wiped her eyes with the back of her hand. "Not really."

"Do you want to talk?"

"I thought you were going to die in that motel room."

"That's what you want to talk about?"

Jill walked toward me, and I opened my arms to hug her. Instead, she grabbed my shirt in her fist. "Don't you ever do that to me again."

"Let it all out."

"That was such a…a messed-up thing. It was out of control and no one else could see what was happening in that room. I had to shoot but you were in the line of fire."

"You told me to get down and I did."

"How could you hear me over all the shouting and screams."

"Marriage has trained me to hear your voice in a crowd."

Jill threw herself on the bed. "I didn't want to shoot that guy but…"

"It was a justified shooting. You heard what Rick Wilson and the attorney said."

"Yeah, well…"

"What did you father whisper to you?"

"He said he'd been stupid and blind. He's proud of me and what I've become."

I hugged her and we lay silently, then she nuzzled my neck. "Mom warned me I'd meet someone like you someday."

"You decided to ignore her warning?"

Jill jabbed me in the ribs with her elbow. "I'm trying to be serious!"

"Sorry."

"When we had 'the talk' she said there'd be boys who'd want to be with me for all the wrong reasons. She told me to be really careful around them."

"That sounds like good advice."

"I was a mess after I broke up with the cowboy. She sat next to me on this bed and told me I'd meet a man who would treat me differently than anyone I'd met before. She said,

269

'Climb on the horse with him. The ride might not go where you'd expect, but you'll never regret the trip.'"

"And…"

"The ride with you isn't going where I expected, but I haven't regretted a second of it."

The End

2019 Bestselling Author
Dean L. Hovey

Dean L. Hovey is the award-winning author of Family Trees: A Pine County Mystery. In addition to his Pine County mystery series, he's the author of the Doug Fletcher series of U.S. National Park Service mysteries and the Whistling Pines series of humorcus cozy mysteries.

Hovey's attention to technical detail and his engaging characters routinely garner positive comments. One reviewer described the Doug Fletcher characters as, "Folks you'd invite over for a beer and conversation."

Dean and his wife split their year between northern Minnesota and Arizona.

BWL Publishing

bwlpublishing.ca

Made in the USA
Middletown, DE
02 November 2021

51542502R00150